Journey to the Middle Meadow

He got up and took it down off the shelf.

It looked like a diary; handwritten and very old.

At first Dad thought it might be private and decided to leave it alone,

but when he flipped the book to the first page, he noticed that someone had written a title there. It was in pencil, as if a child had written it.

It simply said "Edalb."

Cover designed by Frank Geiger with partial AI assist

For my family, who both listened to, and became the stories of my life, but especially for my grandchildren, who I hope will be inspired to cherish their own stories, live them to their fullest, and share them with others.

f. geiger

Table of Contents

ONE

"I've never seen Alaska before!" Adam said. He was excited.

"I have." said Adam's Dad. "It's funny though. That was a really small car too. I wonder if everyone in Alaska drives a small car."

The entire family watched as the little green car with the blue license plate from Alaska passed slowly by the window. The man, who looked more like a college student, smiled at them all as they passed by.

Dad joked, "He doesn't look like a rough, tough, pioneer, does he?"

Mom laughed. "No, he doesn't!"

Adam unbuckled and got up on his knees to get another look at the driver through the rear window. "I bet he has pets that are wild animals. Do you think so Dad?"

It was another trip to Grandpa's farm in Red Hook, New York. Frank and his little brother, Adam, had counted fourteen different states on license plates. Whenever they went up to the farm, they each had a little board that Dad had in the glove compartment to count the various cars they saw. The boards had little plastic slides that covered the state name as you saw on the license plate. Mom always took the boards out, slid up all the spaces that were covered from the last trip, and just before handing them back, slid down the cover over New Jersey.

"Here," she always said. "I did the hard one."

Up until that last car, both Frank and Adam had captured four states each. Alaska put Adam in the lead, and Frank thought that might be the end of the games since nine was a lot.

Frank always pretended to be tired of playing the game and wished that he could have stayed home in New Jersey and just hung out at the pool with his friends, but he had to admit he was impressed when Adam nailed a plate from Alaska. Ignoring his brother and pretending to see something else out the window, he noticed the man in the small car looking right back at him.

"One day," thought Frank, "I'll be the guy away from home, on my own."

They always had fun at the farm, and Grandpa was a good guy and all, but it was summertime, and besides, it was always hot up at Grandpa's farm. Dad had told them that this was a special trip and Frank got the feeling that something was up. Both he and Adam had promised to be good.

Frank had eavesdropped on his parents a few nights ago and got the idea that Grandpa might move back to Mountainside, New Jersey, to live with them. But then yesterday afternoon Frank overheard his mom on the phone talking to his father. Mom was saying that Grandpa had changed his mind, and he wasn't going to "give up." Frank wasn't sure what she meant by that.

This morning, they packed up the car and took off for New York. Frank could tell that the trip wasn't planned. His sister, Paige, had been picked up by friends at the last minute.

Having Grandpa at home would be okay, but deep-down Frank hoped Grandpa would stay on the farm. Once after he and Dad spent the weekend with Grandpa, Frank's father had asked him if he could ever see himself working on the farm over the summer, and maybe learning how to farm.

Frank loved the freedom when he had those acres to himself, even if his brother and sister were tagging along, but he was sure he did not want to be a farmer. Every time he went there it seemed like something was busted, and he never saw his grandfather take a rest.

Farming seemed like a lot of dirty work.

But as he sat in the back seat staring at the hills in the distance, Frank knew that he would miss the farm if Grandpa gave it up. It was a great place for sleigh riding, and they had big bonfires in the winter. And there was more freedom on the farm to explore and hang out than Frank and Adam ever got back home.

They loved to explore in the barn where they had access to a shop of tools and old wood. Once Dad had helped them nail a bunch of boards together for a raft, and the brook that ran through the farm was loaded with fish and frogs.

Paige was too little, but each of the boys had an old pair of sneakers that they left at the farm that they used for walking in the brook.

The more he thought about it, Frank thought maybe he should know more about what was going on with the farm. Adam snapped him out of his daydream by yelling "Maine," but he was sick of counting license plates and declared Adam the winner by sliding his card into the pocket behind his mother's seat.

Even though it seemed like Frank conceded the game to Adam, Adam was sad the game was over and gave his brother a dejected look.

"Anyway," Adam said as he put his card in the pocket as well, "let's keep the cards here and do it again on the way home."

"Sounds good." Frank responded. But was only half listening to Adam as he turned back to the window once again.

Waiting for a moment for his eyes to focus on the small numbers, Frank saw that the little rectangular mile markers on the side of the road told him there were still over thirty miles to go before they reached mile ninety-one on the New Your Thruway. Dad had taught him how to read the markers when they were on their solo trip a few months ago.

Feeling a little dizzy from staring at the posts as they flew by, he turned to face his father in the driver's seat.

"Dad, what's going on? I know that Grandpa sold most of the farm to the power company, but I thought he was keeping the house?" Now that Frank had said the question aloud, it dawned on him that he was actually interested in the answer.

"I mean, and if he owns the house, why does he think he has to move?"

Mom started, "It's complicated-."

But Frank's dad interrupted, "Wait. Let me try." Frank had slid over to the center seat, attached his seat belt, and was now looking at his father through the rearview mirror.

His father continued. “If you want to say that your grandfather sold the farm that’s correct, he did sell about half of his acres, but there’s more to it. The gas company got permission from the government to explore the area for gas and oil. Since your grandfather’s farm was right in the middle of the area, they wanted to look at the most, they bought it.”

Mom raised her hand when she spoke. “Well, they didn’t exactly buy it. They went to court and took it.”

Now Adam got interested and bounced up in his seat. “They sued Grandpa?”

“Not exactly and put your seatbelt back on.” Then dad asked, “Do you guys know what fracking is?”

“I’ve heard of it.” Frank lied.

Dad took a minute to guide the car through the EZ-Pass Lane before he continued. “Basically, fracking is a way of getting gas and oil out of the ground where normally you wouldn’t be able to. They drill a hole, then use water pressure to bring up the gas and oil. Without the water pressure, the oil or gas wouldn’t come up. That’s about all I know about it, and I’m sure it’s more complicated than that.

“But it turns out that the farm is right on top of where they want to look for this oil and gas. I think it’s mostly the gas they are looking for. Not the kind of gas we put in the car at the gas station, but the gas that burns on the stove at home. It’s called natural gas.

So, it’s true that your grandfather did sell them a big chunk of the farm. What we didn’t know is that if the fracking works, they will need a lot of land to put in pipes and stuff. If they do that, I mean if they make a big discovery under the earth, they will need the rest of the farm, including Grandpa's house."

"My house," Mom said.

"Wait." Now Frank was getting interested. "So, I don't get it. Doesn't Grandpa get to stay if he wants?"

"That's where it gets…" and then he looked over at Frank's mom, "complicated."

"Basically, they went to court and told the judge, look, if our tests tell us that there is good oil and gas under this farm, we are going to need the whole thing, and a few other farms as well. They will still pay Grandpa and everyone else the right price, but the farm owners will not have the option to say no."

"That doesn't seem fair." Adam said aloud but meant it to be to himself.

Even Frank was surprised by his brother's unusually wise statement.

"It's not completely fair, but it is sometimes how things work. You know the train tracks you see when we go over the big bridge?" and both boys nodded. "The track that runs along the Hudson River from New York City all the way up? When the government decided that was the right place for the train, they basically told people who owned the land by the river, sorry, but we are putting our tracks here. They paid the people, but the people could not say no, even if they wanted to."

Mom turned back to the back seat and said, "That's why the judge gets involved. Some people are against it. We'll probably see signs protesting."

“Wait, if people are against it, why would we sell it to them. Everyone loves Grandpa!” Frank was getting nervous about the protesters.

“It’s not his fault. A few years ago, your grandfather sold a small piece of land across the road from the farm. He never farmed it, and I think he sold it to put the money aside as college money for you guys. Grandpa thought he was just selling to some guy, not the gas company.”

Dad continued, “Shortly after that sale, he and the whole town noticed the trucks and testing equipment setting up on the property. That’s when everyone heard that there might be gas under the ground. People thought that Grandpa knew he was selling to the gas company, but later in court, the truth came out.

Look, everything will be fine. They may not even find anything. And if they don’t find anything worth digging for, they can’t sell it without offering it back to Grandpa first. I’m guessing they will offer it back to him for less than they paid, so pretty cheap. He could come out of this a winner.”

“For now, your mother and I just want Grandpa to stay with us while this whole thing goes on, so he doesn’t have to worry about it. I think seeing the trucks every day is upsetting.”

Mom shook her head. “There’s something else going on with him. When I spoke to him on the phone, he didn’t sound right. I’m glad we’re going up to check. At least the weather looks great, doesn’t it boys? Oh, look at all the apples!”

This was mom’s favorite part of the trip. On both sides of the highway the apple trees lined the road for about a mile. You could see small apples on many of the trees.

Frank's mind was elsewhere. "I still don't know why Paige was able to stay home and not us."

Mom was quick to turn in her seat. "I will say it one more time. Paige is staying with Aunt Lori and Rachael because we need the room in the car if Grandpa comes back with us, and because she is too little to be left alone at the farm if your father and I are packing and cannot watch her. I do not know what shape anything is in up there and I might be busy getting Grandpa ready to come home."

Then as an afterthought, Mom said, "Thank goodness he has Ralph to look after things if he does come home with us."

To which Dad replied, "Ralph really does run things. Your father doesn't need to be there all the time. But I do know how much he loves this time of year."

Then he turned his attention back to the boys in the back seat. "Come on guys, listen to your mother please, not another word. You know you always have fun up there once you get there. It's a quiet place, but you guys always seem to have fun." Then Dad added. "Maybe you guys could sleep out or something if the weather's good."

Frank looked at Adam and nodded with a little grin, "That'd be cool."

"DOUBLE COOL!" Adam yelled.

"Dad," asked Adam, "Why did Grandpa even sell a piece of the farm it if he didn't want to move? I thought he was rich, anyhow."

"Well," Dad explained. "This may sound weird, but it really started to bother him that he couldn't take care of it. He's been renting the open land out to a local farmer who kept it nice, but that guy sold his farm to the gas company and moved away. Ralph still works the orchard and gets it ready for everyone who comes in the fall to pick apples, but Grandpa figured now would be a good time to not have to worry about so many acres and just take care of his house.

Basically, Grandpa's getting old, and when the oil company started sniffing around, it seemed like the right time. He still has most of the orchard, but the piece the oil company wants really breaks up the property. Since we're never going to live here, maybe it is the right time."

"It's not too late, boys, for you to think about ag school and farming. Your grandfather would be so proud if one of you went to Cornell and got an agriculture degree. The land is waiting for you, and modern farming is becoming a high-tech business."

"It's too hot to be a farmer!" Adam moaned.

Frank nodded his head at his brother, and said, "People that work in tech have air-conditioning. Besides, with my luck, by the time I got out of school, the oil company will own the whole town."

"Oh, well." Mom said, "I'll keep trying." Then she turned out the window to watch her favorite part of the highway.

"But you're right," Dad added, "He doesn't need the money. Which is why I for one, would like him to hang on to the farm while the oil guys go through the test process. There is no reason to run."

With that their father turned back to the road ahead and said to no one in particular, "When I spoke to him last week though, this whole thing was a done deal; I don't know why he changed his mind about taking a little break from it and staying with us. I guess we'll know soon enough."

The boys could never tell how rich Grandpa was, but they knew he was famous. A long time ago he wrote a children's book about these little creatures that he called Orchard Walkers. They were like little weird creatures that lived in the grass. They could talk, but they were really small and green, and shaped kind of like grass, so no one ever saw them. An Orchard Walker spent their days under the apple orchard in tunnels then came out at night when they made little fires.

Frank hated it but he knew the kids at school were jealous when they would tease him and Adam when they saw lightning bugs in the grass. "Look guys... it's the Orchard Walkers in the grass!" Then they would all laugh. It never really bothered Adam as much as it did Frank. The lightning bugs actually did remind him of the Orchard Walkers, or at least it reminded him of the books his grandpa wrote. Mom would always remind him that they were probably a little jealous, and even though they made fun of him and his little brother, in a way, it was proof that Grandpa's stories were well known.

Even knowing that, Frank always thought it was kind of weird to see his grandpa's books in the library or in the bookstore. Some places even sold tee shirts with the Orchard Walkers on them. And the video stores had started selling Orchard Walker video games. He called it kid stuff, which it was. Simple games, but still, it made him wonder how much money his grandfather had? No wonder he was ready to dump the farm.

Frank stared out the window as another orchard came into view, and thought, *I wonder what it's really like to be a farmer?*

Adam was younger, and thought the Orchard Walkers were neat. He had every Orchard Walker sticker, Orchard Walker tee shirt, book or game that came out. When Adam came to your birthday party, you knew pretty much what you were going to get.

As it turned out, Alaska was the best license plate they saw that day, and maybe forever. The rest of the time was spent looking out the windows staring at the mountains and once in a while spotting a deer or horses in a field somewhere.

After going over the Rhinecliff Bridge they stopped for a snack at a little farm that had baby goats in a pen by the parking lot. Dad stayed in the car while Adam petted the goats, and Mom and Frank went into the store. Frank handed Adam some licorice on the way back to the car.

As they were pulling out of the parking lot, Frank pointed out the window and yelled, “Look!”

Everyone looked and saw a “No Parking” sign that someone had painted over. It now said, “No Fracking.”

On their way through town, they saw a few more “Fracking” signs but fewer as they got out of the main town of Red Hook and headed up Route 9 to the farm.

Starbarrack Road leads to the farm and comes down the side of a huge hill that overlooks the whole area. Like he always does, Dad took the long way around in order to stop the car at the top of the hill. Pulling over to the side of the road made a lot of dust, but when it cleared you could see the mountains in the distance that were actually on the other side of the Hudson River.

The orchard was like many apple orchards. Each kind of apple was planted in sections called 'blocks' and all the trees were in straight lines so you could drive a tractor through without hitting any trees. From their car at the top of the hill, the different blocks of trees all had slightly different shades of green leaves and it made the farm look like it was covered with a green blanket with little squares of color.

"I love the rows and colors," Mom said. "This is probably my favorite spot."

"I have to agree." Dad said as he scanned the hills with his eyes. "And don't forget guys," he said as he pointed off to the distance. "Stay off of Old Rusty."

At the mention of Old Rusty, both boys turned their heads. Back beyond the main part of the orchard stood a single tree alone on a hill. They called the tree Old Rusty because it grew yellow rusty looking apples.

"Dad," Adam asked. "Tell me again what kind of apples came from Old Rusty?"

"Roxbury Russets." Came the answer. Then he said, "that trees been here longer than Grandpa."

"We know, dad." Frank said. "You tell us every time."

"Hey mom," Adam called out. "Did you ever climb Rusty when you were little?"

Mom turned around and faked being shocked by the question. "Oh, my NO! It was off limits even when I was young."

As dad pulled away from the curb and started down the hill, Mom shared. “I think Grandpa did once. But that was a long time ago.”

On their way down the hill, they all saw that a new driveway had been put in leading onto the property. There was a huge sign spray painted on an old board that said *Truck Entrance*. It was easy to tell that the new driveway had been used by heavy trucks going in and out of the orchard.

For no reason that the boys could figure out, their mother started to cry a little. “It’s sad,” she said. No one else said anything as Dad drove the car past the barn, the brook, and past the huge mailbox that you could fit a dog in. As the car left the road and started up the bumpy driveway, Grandpa was already standing on the porch steps, waiting for them.

Grandpa was a tall man. No matter how hot it was outside, he always had on a long sleeve shirt. When it was really hot, he rolled up the sleeves, like the way he had them today. With his work pants and boots, he always looked ready to work the farm but hadn’t really done much since he had hired Ralph.

His smile was so sudden when the car stopped; it almost looked like he had been sleeping standing up.

Adam and Frank were excited; it was good to see Grandpa, and good to be at the end of the trip. They both bolted from the car with their backpacks and high fived their grandfather as they ran inside. Then they put their things upstairs in the back room they shared in the farmhouse.

Before the grownups had even got themselves into the house, the boys had changed shoes and ran down the back stairs into the pantry. Grandpa always stocked up on snacks and drinks if he knew they were coming.

"Adam, get a couple of sodas out of the 'fridge. I got the chips." Then Frank yelled to no one, "We're going out!"

After the food raid, they went out the back door and took the path that led to the huge old barn. The farm didn't have any animals, but the barn smelled like horses. The smell was especially strong on a steamy day like today. "I love this smell!" Adam said.

Frank had heard it every time they went into the barn and so said nothing to his brother. Back in the corner on some nails poking out of the wall the boys found what they were looking for. They took down the two fishing nets and went straight down to the brook. They loved walking in the brook and fishing for tadpoles.

"Only you would love the smell of horse manure. That barn is gonna fall down because of that stink one day." Frank said.

Adam said, "How does the barn smell like horses, when there are no horses?"

Not totally ignoring his brother, Frank had to admit he didn't know the answer. After a moment he put an end to the discussion by saying, "All barns smell like horses."

"What do you think is gonna happen to this brook when they start fracking, Frank? Do you think anything will happen?" Adam was starting to worry about the fish and the tadpoles.

"What do you think?" Frank wanted to fish, not talk. "That all happens underground. I don't see how drilling a hole in the ground up on the hill will matter to this brook. Be quiet, look for frogs."

Adam guessed Frank was right, but still, he had seen things on the nature channel where brooks like this got all oily and muddy from too many trucks and all the fish died. He decided by himself that he would try and catch as many fish and tadpoles as he could and move them all down to the larger river, where he hoped they would be safer.

As it turned out, neither Frank nor Adam did very well that first day, seeing just a few tadpoles, and catching none. Every time they chased a tadpole to its hiding place, the mud under the water made it impossible to see anything on the bottom.

After a while, they were called in to wash up for dinner. They took dessert into the living room, but without any apps or cable, nothing was on TV, so they went upstairs to read the new comic books that Grandpa had gotten for them and left on their beds.

Except for Grandpa's writing room, and since there was only one TV that the adults controlled, the boy's bedroom was their favorite place in the house. The door was smaller than most other doors and had an old-fashioned latch on it that you had to lift up to open. When you went into the room, you had to go down two steps. Each bed had a window next to it, and each window looked out onto the farm.

A second door that looked like a closet, actually opened to a small hallway and the back stairs down to the kitchen.

Even though you could see for miles out of each window, the best view the boys liked was looking at the ceiling at night. The ceiling was white, with brown stained boards that made a checkerboard pattern. After everyone was asleep, Frank and

Adam played tic-tac-toe on the ceiling using flashlights. It always started arguments because you could never keep track of which square was already used.

That first night on the farm, Adam fell asleep before he even finished reading the second comic book. Frank was reading using his flashlight but listening as hard as he could to try and hear what his mom and dad were saying to Grandpa. The last thing he remembered before falling asleep is something about Grandpa wanting to stay, and that selling the farm had been a big mistake.

Frank heard his dad. "You're worrying about nothing. We don't even know if they will take the house. I know you've lived here forever, and it was your dad's place, but with the money they're paying you, you could own any farm in Hudson Valley. I suppose we could keep on fighting, but I don't see a way to win this."

"It's not the money John, you know that." Granddad said. "It's not even about the farm."

"Is it about the fracking dad? We saw the signs coming through town." Mom added, "Are the people in town bothering you about the sale?"

"No, no, no, no. Don't let that bother you. It's my darn land to do what I want. My friends understand. It's just that,"

And then just as Frank fell asleep, he thought he heard his grandfather say, "It's complicated."

TWO

In a very restless night of sleeping, Frank had a weird dream about a story he was telling his grandfather. They were both sitting on the front porch stairs and Frank was speaking in rhyme. The story he told his grandfather in the dream came out like a poem even though Frank never wrote poetry or even liked reading it. The dream-speak came from Frank's mouth but did not seem like it was coming from his brain. What he heard himself saying was…

It's true, I really did,
catch an Orchard Walker in the grass.
He tried to trick me by changing his shape.
Thinking I would walk straight passed.

I guess I really got lucky that night.
I had never seen one before.
And the stories I heard were old,
make believe I thought, nothing more.

You never ever see them up close.
Those Orchard Walkers so small they are.
But yesterday when no one was looking,
I trapped one under a jar.

It isn't right to keep them,
at least this much I knew.
But curiosity got the best of me,
and I'd let him go in a minute or two.

He looked just like in the stories,
you would tell us all.
Its long slender body,

green as the grass, and just about half as tall.

Its eyes looked right at me,
his mouth opened like a little "O."
I didn't want to scare him,
and I knew that I would let him go.

So, after a minute of watching,
him and him watching me,
I lifted the jar up, slowly real slow,
and let the little Orchard Walker go free.
But instead of running away,
as I thought for sure he would.
My new little friend bent over,
and picked up a small piece of wood.

The littlest twigs were large to him,
but he put them all in a pack.
He tied them all in a bundle,
and put the pack on his back.

As he went about his work
not taking his eyes off me for long
I could barely hear his voice,
as the Orchard Walker began his song:

"They call me the Orchard Walker
And I have certain Orchard Walker powers.
I pick up all the twigs.
Both the littles and the bigs.
I put them in my pack,
and then I bring them back,
to Edalb and the other Walkers."

And after he finished his song
and his pack was filled as can be.

He leaned backward against his heavy load
and started talking to me.

"I know who you are." he said.
You can imagine my surprise.
"You visit the old man every cold year."
Then he blinked once with both eyes.

"You talk? In English?" I said.
He replied, "Can you keep your word?"
I closed my eyes, and shook my head,
to be sure I heard what I heard.

The Orchard Walker stood and pointed to the house.
"He was once with us, you know.
Oh yes, back when he was a boy,
about 120 years ago."

"He is why we are here.
He holds the meadow twig in his pack.
The middle meadow is where we live.
But without the twig, we'll never go back,
without the twig, we'll never go back,
never go back…
never go back."

His dream interrupted, Frank woke and sat up startled.

"I'LL NEVER GO BACK!" Grandpa was yelling, and Frank jumped right out of bed. *Is it morning already?* Frank thought.

"What's going on?" Adam said in a hushed voice. "I never heard Grandpa yell like that! And what were you dreaming about? You were rolling all over the bed!"

Frank decided not to share the dream. “I know,” Frank looked out the door. “MOM’S COMING!” and he jumped back in bed, pretending to sleep.

Adam fell back into his pillow and pulled up his blanket.

Mom peaked around the door and said, “No, you didn’t wake them, Dad. They were up late last night anyway.”

Grandpa had to bend over to come through the door and then made his way down the steps into the room.

“Good. Let them sleep then, especially this one with the smile on his face.” And he grabbed Adam’s nose between his fingers making Adam jump.

“So,” said Mom, “thought you could fool us, did you?”

Adam could never fake asleep, thought Frank. Oh well, might as well find out what’s going on.

“Why were you yelling, Grandpa,” Frank asked while sitting up in bed. “Don’t ya wanna come and live with us?”

Grandpa spun around and came and sat on the side of Frank’s bed. “Hey, that's not it at all, bud. I just want to keep this place around a little longer, that’s all. Call it unfinished business if you want.”

“Orchard Walker business Grandpa?” Adam asked. “You gonna write another story? Let me read it first this time.”

“No, nothing like that, little buddy.” Grandpa called every kid “little buddy” or “bud.”

"I even had a dream about The Orchard Walkers," Frank said and punched his pillow. "I gotta stop sleeping on these stupid Orchard Walker pillowcases." Then realizing how that sounded, he said, "Oh, sorry Grandpa, you know what I mean."

"Don't be silly, I know you're too old for that stuff. But what about the dream, can you tell me about it?" Grandpa winked at Adam, "Maybe it'll be my next book."

Oh great, Frank thought. Why would he ask me this in front of Adam?

"It was kinda weird Grandpa, I caught one under a jar and it talked to me."

Adam interrupted using his troll voice. "And oh, did it talk like this?"

"Hush a minute, pal," Grandpa waved his hand at Adam. "I want to hear this. What did the little feller say to you?"

"Well," and now Frank felt a little silly. "It said that you were once small like they were and that you had a special twig that they needed to get home. I don't know, not much more, just a stupid dream."

"Hmmm, dreams can be tricky." Grandpa got up and looked out the window. He looked like a giant next to the small door to the room. Then he turned and walked to the stairway that led to the hallway.

"Nope, not enough for a good book. Come on kids, let's get breakfast." Then after a moment he said. "I'll be down in a minute. Save me some sausage."

"Sausage! I knew I smelled sausage!" and Adam flew out of bed and went through the opposite door that took him down the back stairs to the kitchen.

As his grandfather bent down a little to leave the room through the small door at the top of the room's stairs, he turned back to look at Frank. Frank caught him looking at him. He saw the old man's eyes had become wet and shiny. Grandpa winked and smiled but... was he crying?

Before heading for breakfast, Grandpa went into his room at the front of the house. His room was really two rooms with a wide door between them. The larger of the two was his bedroom, and the other was where he worked writing.

The writing room was mostly off limits to the boys and looked like an old library. One wall was completely covered with shelves and old books. On the other side was a huge desk that had a cover that rolled down the front. The cover had never been used though, because Grandpa had so many papers stacked inside and stuck into the little boxes that looked like tiny mailboxes built into the front of the desk.

Grandpa went into the writing room and began looking through some of the Orchard Walker books that he had on his shelf. They were just kids' stories, and of course he knew them all by heart, but something was bothering him.

After flipping through the pages of each book, he placed them back on the shelf and muttered to himself, "Of course it's not here. I would know if it was here. I wrote the darn things."

THREE

Even though the boys promised to stay away from the workers from the gas company, Dad never told them that there would be such neat machines. Up on top of the hill where Grandpa let a local horse owner plant some hay, the men were using a huge crane to unload some big spools of wire. Adam and Frank hid in the tall grass and watched.

Both Frank and Adam jumped when they heard, “Look out!” from one of the men. “The rigging snapped!”

The chain that held one of the bigger spools of cable broke when the crane had it halfway off the truck. It bounced on the ground and slowly started to roll. As it did, one man tried to throw a huge board in front of it, but it rolled right over the board and kept going down the hill.

The hill wasn’t so steep, but as the spool rolled, it kept picking up speed. It bent the tall grass over as it went down the hill making a path that looked almost like a hallway all the way down the hill. The giant spool hit the woods on the far side of the field so hard it sounded like a car crash.

Adam and Frank ran to the top of the hill and looked over to the other side. Some of the men had chased the runaway spool and were running into the woods screaming. The guy in the crane had shut down his engine and was standing outside the cab of his huge machine.

He was looking pretty mad and when he saw the boys, he said, “Man, that's one way to cut down your hay, ain’t it?”

“It’s not ours,” said Frank.

“It’s Timothy!” Adam yelled.

“It’s still called hay,” Frank reminded Adam.

“I know that, but he doesn’t,” Adam quipped.

“I hope Timothy is a nice guy.” The man said. “We may owe him some money.”

Adam was about to correct the man when Frank put his hand in front of Adam and interrupted him. “Timothy isn’t a guy. Timothy is the grass.” Pointing to the nearby field, Frank explained, “This type of grass is called Timothy.”

Now it was Adam’s turn to speak. “I doubt if my grandpa will make you pay for it. We run through it all the time and it bounces back after it rains.”

The man was impressed. “Hey, you kids are pretty smart. But whatever, I told those guys to double up the chain on that big spool, but they don’t listen. That chain that they used was no bigger than a dog leash, and a dog leash is not going to hold a spool that big.”

As Adam looked down the hill at the men, who were still yelling at each other he said to no one, “Man, I would hate to be a dog attached to that thing.”

“Son,” the man in the crane looked down at him. “I don’t know what you would be, but you would no longer be a dog when you got to the bottom.”

“What do you mean, Mister?”

“Well,” and then the man spit. “There’d be pieces, but none of them would look like dog anymore.”

Having said that, the man got back in his truck and began to drive the crane-truck down the hill to get the spool.

Frank took a turn and spit on the ground. “Let’s go Adam, lunch time.”

During lunch, the boys told the family about the runaway wire spool. Dad and Grandpa looked at each other and Grandpa whistled. He was about to say something, but Mom interrupted and said, “That’s not even close to funny. Someone could’ve been hurt. Boys, I believe your father told you to stay away from the workers.”

And now Dad got serious. “Your mother’s right boys, find some other place to play, it’s too dangerous.”

“We were goin tadpolin after lunch anyway,” said Adam.

“Good.” Then Mom joked, “Just watch out for sharks.”

Adam was glad no one was mad at them too much. “If I see one Mom, I’ll bring it home fer supper.”

“Better bring a bigger pail,” said Grandpa, and then he added. “Frank, before you go, can I talk to you for a minute?”

Grandpa got up and waved for Frank to follow. “Wait for me Adam,” Frank called out, and then Frank followed Grandpa all the way upstairs and into the writing room. Frank sat down opposite his grandfather on a smaller chair. Frank thought something was bothering his grandfather and wondered if he was in trouble. He did not get invited into Grandpa’s writing room very often.

“Sorry about the Timothy, Grandpa. And please don’t worry. We were pretty far away when it happened.”

“What? Oh that, forget it, that’s not what this is about. You and I both know that grass will pop up in a few days. I wanted to ask you something about your dream, you know, how you caught the Orchard Walker?”

Frank was surprised by the question but saw how his grandfather was looking at him.

“Yeah, under a jar, like a big jar, but one I could hold with one hand. You remember when we caught that big ole bullfrog and you gave us that big jar from the shed?”

“No,” he laughed.” I mean yes, I do remember the frog, but I don’t mean how you caught it, I want to know exactly what the Orchard Walker said about that twig.”

“Twig?” Frank asked. “The ones he picked up?”

Grandpa leaned forward and waved his hands. “No, no, no. The Orchard Walkers picking up twigs is in every book I wrote. Every kid who reads about the Orchard Walkers knows how they make food from twigs.”

And then the old man folded his hands and rolled his chair slightly closer toward Frank and said, “You mentioned something about a twig I had that keeps the Orchard Walkers from going home. Isn’t that what you said?”

“Oh yeah,” and Frank thought for a minute. “Yeah, something about how you have a special twig. It had a name,” and then it took Frank a minute to recall. “Oh yeah, Meadow Twig, that’s it, that you have the Meadow Twig.”

Frank could tell something was bothering his grandfather, and said, “It was just a dream, Grandpa.” Frank could tell that his grandfather had stopped listening and had even stopped looking at his grandson. Something was going on.

Frank jumped a little when his grandfather suddenly turned to Frank and said, “Frank, I think there is more to it than that.”

“I checked this morning.” He said while waving his hand at the old shelves. In the ray of light that came through the window, Frank could see speckles of dust caused by the huge hand making a small wind. “I went through all my books. I never wrote about the Meadow Twig… not once.”

“What’s that got to do with anything? It was just my dream.” Said Frank as he started to get up from the chair.

“Wait another minute, Frank. Give this old man another minute to explain.” And now it was Grandpa who got up and took something off the bookshelf, placed it in the palm of his hand, and went over to the window looking down at the grass below.

Still looking out the window, the old man said, “Frank, listen to me. Listen to me and believe me.” Then he turned like he was checking to see if anyone else was listening.

A little frightened now, Frank said softly, “I’m listening.”

Seeing for sure that there was no one in the bedroom next door, Frank’s grandfather reached up high, smiled, and put his arms up in the air in a swinging motion making even more dust sparkles float around the room.

Grandpa's head seemed to come out of the foggy dust as he bent over and said, "Frank, it's true. The whole thing is true. Now you know something no one else knows. There is a Meadow Twig, and I have it."

After what seemed like a huge effort to speak, Grandpa took a moment to sit and leaned back in his chair. Looking directly at his grandson, he said, "Wow, I can't believe I actually said that. I never told anyone that before this."

Frank was confused and thought maybe his grandfather was going crazy. After taking a moment to think, Frank said, "Grandpa, it was a dream. It's like all made up. If you really had this Meadow Twig, then that would mean that Orchard Walkers were real. I'm not a kid anymore. They're just stories."

Not sure if Frank was sure what he had just heard, and repeated, "They are just stories, right. Are you saying it wasn't a dream?"

Frank then gave off a nervous laugh, and said, "Wait, what are you saying?"

The old man had a huge grin on his face and was up and bouncing on his toes. "That's right, that's right Frank, and I have never told anyone this before." Then he calmed down and sat again opposite Frank, and whispered, "The Orchard Walkers in the grass exist! They're real!"

Frank just sat there. It sounded like Grandpa was telling the truth. But he was always kidding. "Grandpa, I'm not a kid anymore, I mean gimmie a break." Frank had once heard his mom and dad talking about how maybe Grandpa was *'losing it.'*

Is Grandpa losing it right in front of me? Frank thought.

Grandpa held his closed hand up to Frank's face as if he were holding something. "Look, this is not another story." Now slowly the old man opened his hand, first the thumb, then each hard, wrinkled finger one at a time. When his hand was all the way open Frank looked down. In his hand he held a small stick that seemed to have grown into a circle, about the size of a small ring. Attached to the ring was a small frame made out of dry grass. It reminded Frank of the small backpack the little Orchard Walker was wearing in Frank's dream.

"You have to listen, Frank. Understand your grandpa is not a crazy old man. I need to tell you something. Something I have kept a secret since I was your age."

Frank sat in the old rocking chair while his grandpa told him the incredible story. How when he was a young boy, he was sledding in the hay field, down the same hill that the men were working on today. He said he remembers kneeling on the sled as it went downhill.

"I'll never forget it, Frank. It had rained the night before and the snow had an icy crust on top. Perfect conditions for a fast ride, but before I knew it, the sled started going way too fast so I thought I should jump off. About halfway down the hill, I got so scared I panicked and jumped."

"I know it's going to be hard for you to believe this, but I landed badly. I must have slid on the ice and bumped my head. For a minute I think I must have been knocked out."

Frank saw his grandfather reliving the story in his eyes as the old man rubbed his forehead and pushed back his hair and continued. "I remember waking up, but I don't know how long I laid there. I remember thinking that my mother was there holding my hand. Someone was holding my hand. And when I opened my eyes, there it was."

"Who was it Grandpa?" but Frank was afraid he knew what the answer was going to be. "Was it your dad?"

"Nope, it was an Orchard Walker. Just as real as I am to you today, an Orchard Walker was sitting in the grass holding my hand."

"I realized later that I had accidentally grabbed the Orchard Walker's hand, or it had grabbed mine, and that shrunk me down to their size." Frank noticed how his grandfather's hands were shaking. "You see, when it grabs you… when an Orchard Walker grabs you, you shrink! It was a complete fluke. I guess I was the first person ever to come in contact with them."

Grandpa admitted that at first, he didn't know if he was dreaming or awake. But he went with the Orchard Walker and ended up staying with them for two days. "As we walked, and the grass got shorter and shorter, moving from the tall weeds to the short lawns, we kept getting smaller and smaller."

Frank nodded, remembering from grandpa's books how Orchard Walkers were always half the height of the grass around them. How they eventually got so small they could hide in small tunnels below the apple trees.

Recalling the size of the Orchard Walkers, Frank said, "But you're way too big, even when you were a kid, to grab the hand of -"

But his grandfather cut him off by raising his hand and saying, "Buddy, don't forget how tall the grass is on the side of that hill. Same as it is today. An Orchard Walker even at half the height of the grass would be like," and then he waved his hands around the room seeking an example. Then holding his hand about as high as the chair Frank sat on, he said, "He'd be about as tall as your sister. He was as tall as Paige, and we both were until we started walking together. The whole thing started as an accident."

Grandpa looked down at his hand and touched the little twig with his finger. "An accident caused me to end up with the Meadow Twig, too." Pulling a white cloth out of his pocket like a magician, he wiped his face with the handkerchief and continued.

"That's why I can't leave the farm... The Orchard Walkers need the Meadow Twig to get back to their home on the Middle Meadow; it's kind of like a key. Without it, I don't know what will happen when those men start digging around here. I'm to blame, you see. I'm the reason they are stuck here."

"Wait a minute. Am I supposed to believe this?" By now Frank didn't know what to think and was pacing around the room. "What do you mean they're real... where are they... how come you never told anyone before?"

He motioned for Frank to come to the window and stood behind Frank as they both looked out at the grass. "Out there."

Grandpa pointed to the green lawn in front of the driveway. "They've been living in the grass ever since I left them, taking the Meadow Twig with me. I've tried everything to get this twig back to them but one night I had a dream, just like you. In that dream they told me that only a Notus could put the twig back in its place, since a Notus was the one who removed the Meadow Twig from the Deep Tree."

"Well, after that dream, I tried a hundred different ways to catch one so I could get small again, but catching an Orchard Walker is like catching a shooting star. I guess by the time I started trying... well, I guess I was too old."

Now Frank's grandfather started getting excited. "That's what makes your dream so interesting!" and Grandpa put the little ring of wood back on the bookshelf in a small glass dish. "It's like they're trying to contact you."

A Notus, thought Frank, "this is really weird." He knew that The Orchard Walkers called humans Notus, because to an Orchard Walker, a human was, *not us.*

"How come you never told anyone this?" Frank had walked over and was looking at the little backpack on the shelf.

Grandpa looked up at the bookcase full of papers and children's books and waved his hands across the collection.

"But I did tell you Frank, I told the world… in every book I wrote."

FOUR

After the talk with Grandpa, Frank and Adam had a normal day enjoying the freedom and open doors of being on the farm. He wasn't sure if Adam would even begin to understand, and so Frank kept the story to himself. But later that night Frank decided to tell Adam and see what he thought. After minutes of indecision, he put aside the comic book he was reading and told Adam what went on in the writing room earlier in the day.

"I wouldn't tell you this if I didn't need your help," Frank said as he sat on the edge of the bed. Adam wasn't looking at him and Frank couldn't tell if Adam was listening or not. The younger brother seemed to be concentrating on the cover of his comic. "So, Adam, now you know what I know. Will you help me?"

Adam looked up. "Help you with what? This is crazy. You have a dream about writing poetry, and now Grandpa tells you that the Orchard Walkers are real. Do you believe him? Did you ever think that he was just telling you another story? He is a writer! He tells stories for a living. Why would he tell you and not tell us all? You remember what dad said. Old people sometimes get confused."

"I know," Frank conceded, "but I believe him. The main reason we are here is because he won't leave the house. And he won't leave the house because The Orchard Walkers are here. And they won't leave because of the twig."

Frank flopped back into his pillow and then said to himself, *'I do believe him, don't I?'*

Staring at the ceiling, Frank continued. "I know… I sound as crazy as you think I am. But here's something else. What do we have to lose by trying to give the twig back? We are always looking for something to do. Let's make a plan and do this thing! Grandpa was our age when he said he caught one. If he can do it, or did it, we can do it."

Hoping to be taken more seriously, Frank sat up in bed and stared at his brother. "But to be safe, we'll keep it a secret, so no one thinks we're crazy."

Now Adam sat up and looked straight at his brother. It appeared to Frank that Adam was beginning to believe him, and his face seemed more serious when he said, "Question. If this is all true, why don't they walk up to Grandpa and just grab him? If they need this twig so bad why not just come and get it? If what you say is true, once they grab him, he would become small, and he could just hand it over to them."

"I don't know, but I asked him that," Frank said. "We're too big, and they are too small. They're like the smallest blade of grass on the lawn, even half that size. How would they grab you? And if they did, they might get hurt as you shrunk."

Frank went on. "The main thing Grandpa said was that he thinks it only works in one direction. You have to catch them, or nothing happens. We know they're fast, and they're basically invisible in the grass. And don't forget the tunnels. That part of his books is true, too."

Grandpa said like we see lightning bugs at night, but never during the day. It's the same with the Orchard Walkers, I guess."

"He said that when he fell off the sled, he got lucky, or unlucky depending on how you look at it. They are always moving and trying to stay hidden they wouldn't stand still for you."

"They've basically been living in the orchard since Grandpa was a kid. Living in tunnels under the trees during the day and coming out at night to gather twigs to make food-coals. Unless we can get them the Meadow Twig to open the Deep Tree, they are stuck here."

Trying his best to convince Adam to believe him, Frank continued and said, "Grandpa says if the Deep Tree doesn't open before the gas company starts ripping up everything, the Orchard Walkers could be destroyed."

"Wait," Adam started to speak. "I just thought of something. If all of this is true, then where is this tree called the Deep Tree? In the book Grandpa talks about this protected..."

Frank spoke up interrupting his brother. "It has to be Old Rusty; you know that single apple tree way back in the orchard that we are not allowed to climb on? I think that's the Deep Tree. I've been thinking about it. I think that's the tree that takes the Orchard Walkers home.

Adam knew he couldn't see Old Rusty from their window, and it was dark out anyway, but he went to the window and looked. He, Paige, and Frank had been told over and over to stay away from it.

Grandpa had told them it was actually not his tree, but that the ground it grew on was actually owned by Cornell University and was state property.

The boys had heard the story almost every summer while visiting the farm. Thinking he knew every kind of apple that grew in the world, Grandpa had picked some apples from the tree and brought them to the university to find out what kind of apples they were. He was stumped but Cornell was famous for helping New York apple farmers, so they were happy to see if they could help him.

When he placed the yellowish-brown apples on the table in the agriculture lab at Cornell, the scientists got extremely excited. They took their grandfather to the field behind the lab and showed him three long rows of apple trees.

The man who gave the tour explained that the Cornell Center for Agriculture and Life Sciences had an orchard of every variety of apple tree in the United States. The three rows of trees behind the building were like a living museum of trees. They had every apple tree variety, except one.

After the tour was over, the man explained that the apples that Grandpa had brought were called Roxbury Russet and the tree on Grandpa's farm was the only one known to be alive. The scientist explained that the tree needed to be protected, and even the governor of New York came to the orchard and declared the tree a state landmark.

Adam remembered something about how the original seeds were brought over by the Pilgrims. No matter what happened to the farm, Grandpa explained it would never be cut down, and even though Adam hated not to climb it, he understood why.

But man, he thought. If ever a tree needed to be climbed.

Adam muttered to himself, *'so the Deep Tree is the old Rusty?'* and saw that Frank was nodding towards his brother. Frank could see that Adam was starting to understand.

“So, now we stop trying for tadpoles, and start catching Orchard Walkers? I don’t even know if I can believe you.” Adam had moved over to Frank’s bed and was looking down at his big brother. “Dream again, little buddy.” Adam said in his troll voice. “Maybe tonight, Tinkerbelle will come see us.”

Frank’s pillow hit Adam in the chest right before Frank tackled him. They both fell to the floor, laughing a little too loud.

“Guys!” It was Dad. “Hit the lights and hit the beds, will ya, it’s late.”

“Okay!” Adam yelled from under Frank. “Get off of me ya big Notus.”

Frank stood up and went back to bed, smacking the light off with his pillow as he went by the switch. As he went by the window he stopped and turned. Putting his face up against the glass created a fog that Frank wiped away with his hand. After staring for a minute, he put his face right up to the glass to be certain he was seeing clearly. “Adam, you gotta see this.”

“What?” Adam came over with his pillow in front of him for protection just in case it was a trick. “Who’s out there, Dumbledo-Ohmygosh!”

“Shhhh! Dad will hear us… do you see what I see?”

Outside the house, on the lawn, were hundreds of little lights. It looked like every firefly in the world had come to Grandpa’s to visit.

“I never saw so many lightning bugs,” Adam said.

“No, look again, nothing is moving... it’s the Orchard Walkers, just like Grandpa said.”

Sure enough, the Orchard Walkers had all come up from underground and made their coal fires for the night. The boys watched for a while, knowing they wouldn't see anything but blinking lights, but hoping to anyway. After leaning on the windowsill long enough to put dents in their hands, they laid back in bed. Neither of them spoke. They were thinking.

Adam lay awake in the dark. Like a full moon, the light from the lawn gave the ceiling a glow. As the specs danced across the boards that made up the squares, the ceiling became like a city as seen from far away in space. Adam was thinking about how cool it was that an Orchard Walker could be real, and how cooler it was that that only he and his brother knew. "You know," he said, thinking of the kids back in New Jersey who teased him, "if I caught one of those Orchard Walkers, I'd be famous."

It took a moment for Frank to answer. "Adam, if you caught an Orchard Walker and gave them back the key to the Middle Meadow, you'd be a hero."

Still staring at the ceiling and thinking about it all, Adam said, "Yeah, this is the neatest secret we ever had."

Frank was thinking this too, but he was also thinking about how he could get the Meadow Twig back to the Orchard Walkers before the gas company came through and destroyed the place. Eventually both boys fell asleep without another sound.

FIVE

Once again, during an uncomfortable night of sleep, all of that day's events fell into Frank's dreams as if someone had poured out a box of memory crayons and mixed them all up. Frank dreamed that he saw his grandfather sledding down a hill and being chased by the big spool of wire. Then, just as the spool was going to land on top of Grandpa, a dog with a huge leash pulled him out of the way. After the spool crashed into the woods, he looked up the hill and saw the men standing by the crane laughing.

Just as the sun started to light the room, Frank woke up sweating, wiped his face on his blanket and propped himself up on his elbow and stared at his brother.

Adam was asleep. He turned and looked out the window and saw that the sun was still hiding behind the hills.

"Adam," Frank said as he quietly went over and shook his brother. "Adam, come on, I know how we can get the Meadow Twig back to the Orchard Walkers... Adam, are you up?"

Grumbling, Adam said, "I guess I am now; what time is it?" Then he rolled over to face the old clock on the desk. "Frank, it's only five o'clock in the morning! What happened? Did you have a bad dream, or something?"

"Quiet! Don't wake mom! No, I didn't have a bad dream, but I do have a plan. I think I know how we can save the Orchard Walkers. But we have to do it now, before anyone wakes up."

Grumbling, Adam got dressed. While he did, Frank tiptoed across the hall and went into Grandpa's writing room using the hallway door. No way was he going in through the bedroom. He could hear Grandpa snoring and was careful not to make any noise. *STUPID FLOOR!* he yelled to himself every time it creaked.

After making his way over to the shelf, he reached up and took the Meadow Twig. Before leaving the room he gently pulled open a desk drawer, pulled something out, and went back into the bedroom.

Adam was tying his shoes. "I don't know what you're thinking, but this is nuts." Adam stood up and faced his brother.

"I'm nuts, and you decide this the morning to wear an Orchard Walker Tee shirt." Frank handed the twig, which was still attached to the small backpack, to Adam. "Here," he said, handing his brother a small pin. "Pin this on my back."

Adam gave Frank an angry look, and said, "I thought the shirt would bring us luck. Wow, is this it? The Meadow Twig? It's so small. How did it grow in a perfect circle like that?" Adam held it up to the light and looked through the ring of bark. "Do you think it has magical powers? It's so cool."

"Hey," Frank was getting anxious. "We have to move if we're going to do this without anyone stopping us." He took back the safety pin and opened it. "Quick wasting time and pin it to my back."

As Frank turned around, Adam started pinning the pack on Franks back but stopped and said, "Hey, how come you get to wear the little backpack?"

Frank didn't turn around. "Simple. I had the dream, and I have the idea on how to get this back to them."

Adam thought for a moment and smiled. "And you are the one that will end up in trouble. Okay, you can wear it." And with that, the two boys quietly went down the back stairs of the house. They both stopped at the pantry but the door was closed and so they decided getting something to eat would make too much noise.

After making it out of the house, they crossed the rear yard as the still sleeping sun made it just bright enough to be daylight. Adam still did not have a clue about his brother's plan as he followed him and the small backpack into the barn.

"All right, Frank, what's the big plan? What do we need in the barn, the nets?

"No, trust me; I know what I'm doing. I don't know why I know; I just know."

Frank walked to the corner of the barn and took Grandpa's sled down from the wall where they left it last winter.

"The sled, in September?" Adam tried not to laugh in case someone in the house would hear. "Frank, look at my tee shirt again... it's basically summer, remember?"

Frank decided to ignore his brother mocking him. "I remember how Grandpa caught that Orchard Walker, and I'm gonna do the same thing, and we don't need snow to do it, I think this is really gonna work!" And with that Frank walked out of the barn with the sled under his arm. It was heavy, but he knew if he dragged it by the rope, it would make a lot of noise.

Adam really thought Frank looked funny as he carried the sled up the hill walking between the tall blades of the grass, but he followed him. “I could really go for a Pop Tart.” It took a few minutes to reach the top of the hill.

The boys had returned to where they had seen the workers the day before. Frank stopped and put down the sled. “Adam look, there’s Orchard Walkers in the grass.”

Adam spun around. “I don’t see anything. What’re you gonna tell me now, you got some kind of Orchard Walker vision?”

“No, look at the grass. It’s moving like the wind is blowing, but there’s no wind. I think they’re watching us.”

Adam looked out across the field. It was true. Even though there was no wind, every once in a while, a small patch of the field would move back and forth, like something small was running through the tall blades. That made Adam a little nervous but at the same time, he was getting excited.

“Should we be afraid? Maybe we should be a little bit afraid.” Adam backed up a bit until he was standing next to his brother and put his foot up on the sled. “Okay, I believe you. But how are you gonna sled down this hill, even with a running start, you’re only gonna go two feet at the most and then face-plant in the rocks.”

“I’m not gonna sled down this hill, I’m gonna sled *up* it, and you’re going to help me do it. Let’s start by getting some of this wire unwrapped.”

Adam hesitated, but then worked with Frank as both boys went to work on one of the smaller spools of wire the work men had taken off the truck after hauling the large spool that crashed into the woods back to the work site. As they began to unwind the wire off the spool, Frank explained his plan.

"Here's what we're gonna do. When we get enough of this wire off the spool to reach down to the woods at the bottom of the hill on that side," Frank spoke as he pointed towards the woods. "Then I'm gonna tie the wire to the sled and get on.

"When I give you the signal, you knock out this block of wood under the spool on this side." Frank said, pointing now to the barn. "That will make it roll down the hill on this side. When the wire gets tight, it'll start pulling me up the hill and over the top. As I cruise along, if I see an orchard Walker, I'll grab him."

Adam looked down towards the bottom of the hill and then back up the hill, then down at the barn, then back at his brother and asked, "Then what?"

"I'll give them back the Meadow Twig."

Adam couldn't help giggling as he said to Frank, "That's nuts! Even if I could knock out this block, and even if it rolls fast enough, you're not gonna see an Orchard Walker with his hand out hitch hiking. They're too fast and always hide from humans, remember?"

"Yeah, but this time I think they'll be waiting for me." Frank said as he recalled his dream from last night. "I just feel like they are. And if it doesn't work, we ditch the sled, run back to bed, and forget it."

"I say we forget it now, it's not gonna work, and even if it does, what am I gonna tell Mom and Dad if you end up getting small with the Orchard Walkers?" Adam could not believe he was talking like this.

“I don’t know... tell Grandpa, he’ll understand. Besides, I only expect to be with them for a minute and give them the twig. Listen Adam, suppose this stuff is for real, and these gas guys come back and rip up the farm and kill all the Orchard Walkers? Don’t you think it’s worth at least a shot?”

“Mom and Dad won’t like this,” Adam said.

Frank knew he was close to getting his brother to agree and said something he knew would hit Adam in the heart. “If it works, Grandpa can stop worrying.”

Adam looked down the hill at the house and thought for sure this was gonna cost him something. From where he stood, he could see the window to his grandfather’s bedroom. He closed his eyes for a moment, then turned and looked up at his brother, “Help me find something to bang out this block of wood.”

SIX

After finding an old sledgehammer by some boxes of huge nails, and giving it to Adam, Frank carried the sled down to the bottom of the hill. Twice Frank had to go back and get the end of the wire after it pulled away from his hand.

Once he reached the bottom, the wire came out of the spool like a giant slinky that ran all the way down the hill to the sled. Frank was able to sit on the sled, wrap the wire around and through the front of the sled and twist it around like a twist-tie.

At first Frank sat up on the sled then after thinking about it, laid down on his stomach and grabbed the wooden handles. “Here goes nothing,” he said, and then looked up and waved to Adam.

After seeing Frank wave, Adam took the hammer and started hitting the block of wood that held back the big spool. “This isn’t gonna work,” he mumbled.

Adam had a little trouble swinging the big hammer, but soon the wood block started to move and finally with one last blow, the block of wood cleared away from the spool.

The weight of the hammer made Adam lose his balance and he almost fell. Once he straightened himself out, he looked at the spool. It didn’t move.

“It won’t move, I got the wood out, but it won’t roll!” Adam yelled down to Frank as loud as he could, taking care not to yell loud enough to wake anyone up.

"What?" said Frank. "Give it a push or something!"

Adam turned back to the wire spool, which was almost as tall as him. Adam muttered to himself, "yeah right, a superhero couldn't push this thing out of the way."

But then, even before he could touch it, the spool started to move, at first very slowly, and then it began to roll down the hill.

"It's going! It's going!" and this time Adam was yelling.

Frank couldn't really hear what Adam had said, but he realized something had changed and so he jumped back on the sled. He saw the wire get pulled straight, and then got tight. Ever so slowly, the sled started moving up the hill.

"Wow, it's working" he said to himself. "Is this as fast as it gets?"

But Adam saw it differently. The spool, which began moving really slow, started picking up speed as it hit the down part of the hill. He also saw that as it made its way down the hill, it was wrapping the wire back up in spool even faster than it was moving. He turned to check on his brother and saw that Frank had gotten to the top of the hill just about when the spool was halfway down the other side, and even though Frank and his ride had started slow, Frank was moving really fast now.

It was hard to control the sled. It seemed to go wherever it wanted no matter how Frank tried to keep it straight. It was all Frank could do to hang on. By the time Frank got to the top of the hill, he had forgotten about looking for the Orchard Walkers and was looking for a safe place to land. Just ahead, Frank saw a safe place to jump off, but just as the sled entered the downslope of the Timothy field, something landed on his back.

Adam, watching this whole thing, was scared and excited all at the same time. When he saw his brother reach the top of the hill, he did what he almost always did when they were sleigh riding in the wintertime. He ran alongside his brother and jumped up on top of Frank and made a double-decker ride out of it.

"Get off me Adam, what are you doing?" Frank yelled.

"I'm going with you," and then "uh, oh!"

The huge wheel of wire hit a rock at the bottom of the hill, was knocked to the side and was now heading directly for the barn. And as if that weren't enough, the wire was running out really quick, and both boys realized at the same time that in another minute, they would be wrapped around the spool too.

"We have to jump off!" Frank yelled. But it didn't matter. Before he could finish the warning, the sled hit a rock in the field tossing the boys like hackie-sacks up and over the hedge row of Timothy where they disappeared into the field.

SEVEN

The spool and the attached sled kept going and when the spool hit the barn side it did not stop as it crashed right through the old wooden front wall. The sled caught up with the spool somewhere in the middle of the barn and then the twisted mess of wood, wire, and sled crashed through the back wall of the barn, rolled through a flat field of dandelion flowers and with a huge splash landed in the brook. The whole mess came to rest on the opposite side of the little waterway up against the clay bank.

The sled, now a broken bundle of splinters and steel, hung on the back side of the spool, dangling from Frank's wire knot.

The sled was still swinging back and forth when Grandpa, Mom, and Dad, all hit the front porch of the house running toward the barn. "What the heck was it?" yelled Grandpa. "Sounded like a plane crash!"

All three adults went in the barn through the hole that the spool made, and all three of them went out through the hole in the back. Dad was first to see the spool in the brook. "Would you look at that," he said, glad it wasn't a plane after all.

"Darn it, I told them fellers to brace those things yesterday. Somebody could've gotten themself killed!" Grandpa looked around. "Lynn, just look at this mess… incredible!"

Mom had been quiet up to this point. "I can't believe something like this could happen two days in a row. "Thank goodness the boys are in bed, later on this morning they'd be fishing in this brook."

"Hey Dad, take a look." The boy's father had used some of the stones in the brook and had made his way to the other side. He turned to face his father-in-law and was standing next to the spool. The sides were splintered a bit, and bits of hay were tangled up in the wire. There was even a piece of barn siding sticking out from the tangled mess.

"You can kiss your old sled good-bye." And with that he pulled it from around the back side of the spool to show the damage. "It must've gotten tangled up in the wire as it went through the barn, it's all busted up."

"That's the least of it," said Mom, "nobody's about to take out the sled and go sliding down the hill today, anyway."

Hearing his daughter talk about sledding down the hill, Grandpa took a closer look at the ruts made in the grass by the out-of-control spool. Then it hit him, and he turned to his daughter as if struck by lightning. "Oh my gosh! Oh no!" But before anyone could ask him what was wrong, he went racing back to the house.

EIGHT

Even though Grandpa got a head start running back to the house, the boy's parents got to the house just as Grandpa reached the front stairs. The old man's first stop after racing up the front stairs was the writing room; and he went straight to the bookshelf.

"Please be there," he muttered under his breath. But it was not. He looked at the shelf for the Meadow Twig and small grass pack. He pushed aside some books and papers but saw that it was gone. He spun around when he heard footsteps coming into his room. He was hoping it was the boys.

"Dad," Mom had a really worried look on her face. "Are the boys in here with you?"

The old man dropped down into the rocking chair shaking his head. Dad reached for the old-fashioned phone on the table and said to his father-in-law, "Albert, I'm calling the police."

"Wait," Grandpa hoped this couldn't be happening. "I think I know where they are. This can't be happening, I mean, everything will be fine but…" Mom and Dad both waited for the old man to make sense.

He continued, "They're with... and please understand I didn't mean for this to happen, but I think they might be with the Orchard Walkers."

Slowly Dad put the phone down. He looked over at Mom who was trying to speak, but nothing came out. "What the heck are you talking about? The kids are missing Dad, what's going on?"

He could see that something was bothering his wife's father now. "Are you okay, do you need a doctor? What do you know about the boys? Where can I find them?"

Grandpa stood up, "Give me five minutes and let me tell you something. No, I don't need a doctor. I think I know where the kids are. We can call the sheriff, but first listen to me."

Mom took Dad's hand as they both sat on the bed listening to the whole story. Of how Grandpa was taken in as a child by the Orchard Walkers, and how now he thinks Frank and Adam are with them, returning the Meadow Twig.

Dad tried to contain himself even though he thought the old man had lost his mind. He thought, "Had all these stories he wrote gone to his head? Does he know what's real and what's not?

It was easy for him to think that the old man was wrong because this story, Dad was thinking, could not be true.

"All right let's stay calm," Dad said. "Let's say for a minute, this is all true. You were little once like these little green guys; you kept it a secret for sixty years and now my boys are little too. As incredibly impossible as this all sounds to us, I have to ask you Albert, because after all, you are the expert, where would they be right now?"

Lynn didn't like how her husband was talking to her father, as if maybe Albert was living a fantasy, but she had to admit she was leaning more toward her husband's side of the story.

"Think Dad!" Now Mom was crying. "I want them home now."

“Well,” said the old man as he rubbed his chin, “if it worked... if they really caught one, I’d say they would still be in the hay field up on the hill.”

NINE

Before he could finish, the boy's father ran out of the room, down the back stairs, and headed out to the field calling for his sons. He had second thoughts about going up the hill and decided to take a second look in the brook.

Earlier it hadn't dawned on him that his boys may be hurt and lying in the water somewhere. After taking a few minutes to check around the bank of the small stream, he was glad that he didn't find them there. The water in this spot was a favorite of the boys and only a foot or so deep, so after a quick look, he saw that it was empty and then turned his attention to the barn.

After working his way back up the hill following the path made by the giant wheel, he came to a place where the tracks made by the sled were much deeper, and they stayed that way all the way up the hill.

"Look at this," he said to the boy's mother, who with Grandpa, had followed him up the hill and were looking around the field. "If Adam and Frank were riding the sled down the hill, they got off here, where the tracks get lighter."

Grandpa kicked at a rock sticking out of the ground right about where the deeper tracks ended and said, "Or got bumped off."

"But where are they?" Mom said. She was really starting to worry now.

"Maybe they're hiding," Dad said. "Afraid we're gonna be mad at them."

Mom shook her head, "I just want to see them. They never get up this early."

Seemingly speaking to no one in particular, Albert spoke softly as he said, "It's possible we can't see them, because they're down in the grass." said Grandpa, even though he was hoping it wasn't true.

Both Mom and Dad just stared at the old man. "Look," Dad finally said. "Let's do a quick check of the entire length of the brook first, then the woods, under the front porch, any place where you think they might be hiding. I'll do the brook and meet you both back at the house in ten minutes or so."

The three went scouting for the boys. Once again, the boy's father went into the barn and out the back. When he was sure he was out of sight he took his cell phone out of his pocket and placed a call to the local sheriff.

Hearing that two boys were missing was big news in the sheriff's office. Anything actually would be news so early in the morning, but after hearing about the barn the sheriff quickly came to the same conclusion as the boy's father, the boys were probably hiding.

"Please stay calm, sir. I'm going to give Billy a call. He has a good dog that I swear can find things even when they're not there. One sniff of the boy's sock and he'll be on the trail, yes sir. If not hiding, I'm sure the boys are just out exploring in the woods. Give me about a half hour to put it together. I know the place. You take a look around and stay calm; they couldn't have wandered too far."

TEN

Back up the hill, Adam was lying on his back feeling his forehead. "Oh man, what happened?" Feeling something wet, and looking at his hand, Adam said, "oh man, I'm bleeding, Frank, my head is bleeding!"

"Let me see, let go of my hand." Frank tried to get up to take a look at his brother's head. He felt for sure if Adam were hurt, he would be blamed but good.

"You let go, I'm trying. What the?"

"Oh my gosh Adam. Look, we did it... we're small.... I think."

Both boys noticed at the same time that they were not alone and jumped up at the same time. "I see it. Oh man, we're in big trouble now. Will it hurt us? Why won't it let go?"

Sure enough, right between Frank and Adam, holding both their hands, was an Orchard Walker. It looked just like in the books Grandpa wrote, but this one was as big as they were. The boys were scared and stood with their mouths open staring at the thing before them, which stared right back.

The pack that was pinned to Frank's back was now as big as a regular backpack. The small safety pin was enormous, or it was the same and they really did shrink. Adam was feeling funny and thought he might pass out.

"Frank, we did wake up today, right? I mean, this isn't just a dream?"

“Notus, Notus.” The funny green creature was talking to them and looking back and forth from Frank to Adam.

Frank was feeling a little braver and decided to speak first. He shrugged his shoulders and turned to the green creature that continued to keep a firm grip on their hands. “I have the twig, the Meadow Twig. If you let go of me, I’ll give it to you. We did this to bring you the twig, do you understand?”

Both Frank and Adam were startled when the walking leaf-like creature spoke back. “No, don’t let go.” To the boy’s surprise, the Orchard Walker sounded similar to the troll voice Adam teased Frank with the night before. “If you do, you will get big again, and I will lose you. It would not be good. Walk with me to Edalb, Edalb calls to you.”

“I don’t hear anything....” Adam tried to listen to a far-off voice.

Then he said, “Does it feel like we are walking…”

“Through one of Grandpa’s books?” Frank answered by finishing the sentence.

It seemed completely safe, so they followed the Orchard Walker while holding its hand. As they walked through the field of tall grass, it was hard to see anything because the grass was about twice as big as they were, but when they crossed over the area that was crushed by the spool, Adam got a glimpse of the hole in the barn wall.

“Frank, look what you did to the barn! Hey, I see Grandpa running back to the house, I wonder why he’s running back to the house? Hey, Grandpa!” Adam shouted.

"He can't hear you. What do you mean, what I did? We both did it!" But Frank knew that it really was his entire fault and wished he never had this stupid idea. "I bet they're mad. Oh man, I bet they're looking for us. What was I thinking?"

At the edge of the field where the hay met the grassier field, the Orchard Walker told them to jump. As soon as they landed in the grass, they shrunk down again so that the lawn was once again about two times taller than they were.

"Cool!" said Frank.

"Not cool! I'm scared," said Adam. "We're really small now. I can't see a thing. I feel like I'm in the fur of a giant green animal." Adam motioned to Frank with eyes. "Except I can see them. Oh my gosh… speaking of green!"

Sure enough, more Orchard Walkers were in the grass now with them. One of the Orchard Walkers came over and put a little wreath of grass over Frank's head. When he did, the first Orchard Walker let go of Frank's hand. Nothing happened. "Look Adam, the necklace must be keeping me small!" Frank guessed.

When the Orchard Walker gave Adam a wreath, he looked at his shirt and saw the Orchard Walker on it. His mouth went into the shape of a perfect O, but nothing came out. As Adam stood there, the creature moved in so close Adam thought he was going to kiss the image on his shirt, but it never touched him but gave off a *"hmm"* sound as he stood back.

Adam started to laugh. "You want the shirt? My Grandpa gave it to me. It's you guys!"

Frank watched and was going to protect his brother but then saw that the Orchard Walker was simply curious. "He doesn't want your shirt. They want this twig on my back. Hey Adam, you really did hurt yourself, your head is still bleeding."

Adam reached up and felt the bruise. When he looked at his hand his fingers were all red. He sat down. "It'll be all right." Then, turning to the group of new friends, he said, "hey, you guys look funny, we never see you up close, just in the books Grandpa wrote… or in a video."

It really was the first time anyone had seen an Orchard Walker since their grandfather was with them so many years ago. Standing just about as tall as the boys are now, all of the Orchard Walkers had a similar green color. The grass-green shades seemed to melt into the background. Even though they were standing so close, they seemed to fade away and then return. Frank was thinking *no wonder it's impossible to see them.*

Their small black eyes were surrounded by large white ovals. Adam had always told Grandpa that the eyes on an Orchard Walker made them look like they were surprised except the expression never changed. The boys noticed that when the eyes closed or blinked, the eye almost disappeared, since their eyelids were green as well.

The Orchard Walkers had a little mark for a nose, like a small triangular bump, and hands and feet that looked a little like baseball mitts. Some had packs on their backs like Frank had. A few, like the Orchard Walker that caught the boys in the field, had light green blades of grass wrapped around their waists. At least that's what the belts looked like.

The Orchard Walker that had been staring at Adam had both a belt and a pack. It seemed like he could not take his eyes off of the tee shirt.

Adam guessed what the Orchard Walker was thinking. "You look funny to us, too. We only get to see you from drawings."

The Orchard Walker that caught Frank and Adam in the field spoke next. Adam noticed that as he moved, the blade around his middle shimmered and almost appeared wet.

"What is a video? He asked. Both boys spoke at once as they tried to explain about their grandfather who wrote stories about the Orchard Walker clan and how they are famous, but no one really believes in them. From the expressions given by the creatures, it was fairly clear that they did not seem to understand the boys very much.

"Notus was great," said the one with the grass belt. "He saved the clan."

The two boys looked at each other. Frank noticed more blood coming down Adam's neck. "Adam, you have to go home and let Mom look at that bump, you're still bleeding. I'll be home right after I give Edalb the twig."

"No, I want to go with you, it's not that bad, really Frank, let me come, too." But Adam could not hold back the tears in his eyes. The cut really hurt badly, and the blood was scaring him.

"Look, go home, and tell Mom and Dad I'm okay. I'll be home in a few minutes. You can't see it, but believe me, you need to get that looked at."

Adam thought that his brother was going to take a better look at his cut, but instead, Frank pulled at the grass ring from around Adam's neck ripping it right off his brother. Adam heard his brother whisper, "I'm really sorry, Adam." And then everything got weird.

Right away Adam shot up to his regular height falling to the side. Startled by his sudden change of size, he froze in place. Standing and regaining his balance, Adam took a giant step away from where his brother was. Adam looked back at the ground searching for the spot where he just was and saw nothing.

Getting down on his hands and knees, Adam bent down looking for any sign of where he just was. As he did, blood ran down his cheek and dripped on the grass. Frightened, he turned and ran toward the house.

ELEVEN

"Adam! John look, it's Adam." Mom was on the porch of the house looking out over the yard when Adam seemed to come out of nowhere running toward her. She ran down the steps as his father and grandfather came out of the house. "Oh Adam, where have you been?" she said as she grabbed him and hugged him.

"John, he's bleeding, get him into the house. Adam, where's your brother? Is he hurt?" Mom asked.

"No, he's out there with the Orchard Walkers. I was too." Adam was barely able to contain himself. "Grandpa it worked, they really are real, they really are real. Frank has the twig and he's taking it to Edalb-."

But before he could finish, the porch door slammed behind him as his father carried him into the kitchen where his cut was cleaned, and then his folks took him up to bed. It was still early in the day. After he calmed down, he told them all about what he and his brother did. Dad didn't seem too mad and sat at the side of the bed with his hand on Adam's back.

Adam wanted to share more about where exactly Frank would be, but all he could say was, "in the lawn. He's down in the grass." Exhausted by the events of the early morning, he was able to explain falling off the sled and hitting his head but fell asleep before much could really be learned. His mother and father closed the door to his room behind themselves, and just held each other outside in the hallway. They were interrupted by a squeal of tires out on the main road, then they heard cars coming fast down the driveway.

Grandpa had been looking out the window. "John, Lynn, come down here. The police are here. Who called the sheriff?"

Lynn looked at her husband, who looked up at the ceiling and said, "Yeah, that would be me."

When they got outside the sheriff and his men had made their way to the side yard and were looking at the barn. The sheriff had on a light brown sheriff's uniform. Under the brim of his matching baseball cap style hat, he hid his eyes behind large mirror sunglasses.

The two men that came out of the other car did not have uniforms and looked like they had been dragged out of the hardware store on the way out of town. The sheriff took off his cap and tapped it against his leg when everyone joined him on the lawn.

"Sheriff," mom called to him. "Could I ask you to step off the lawn? I don't want you to crush… I mean we just fertilized. It might ruin your shoes."

The sheriff spun around to face them and as he stepped forward onto the gravel and pointed his cap at the barn off in the distance. "Good morning, folks. What in the world happened here? It looks like a plane crash. Say, those kids come home yet?"

"Good morning sheriff, I'm John Webster, this is my wife, Lynn. I called you this morning. Oh, and this is my father-in-law…"

"Don't bother, I know who he is, heck, everybody knows Albert B. Cole. The ABC Farm has been around these parts a while at least." He passed his cap to his left hand and shook hands with the old man with his right. "You write those books about those little critters. Apple Walkers or something like that, anyway, my grandkids know all about them."

Using his cap again to point back at the barn, he asked them one more time. "Now, what the heck is this all about? You find yer boys?"

Grandpa was a little nervous and began to say, "We'll find them soon enough, thank you sheriff, we won't need you here today, sorry for any inconvenience."

John interrupted and said, "What my father-in-law is saying sheriff, is that we have reason to believe that this mess you see here may have been the handiwork of the boys in question, we haven't quite got the full story yet. But our youngest, Adam is now upstairs in his room." Faking his anger, he added, "We have reason to think that Frank may be hiding, waiting until we aren't mad anymore."

"Yeah, I see what you mean. If I was that rascal, and made all this mess, I'd shrink out of sight, too!" The sheriff waved the other men back into the cars. "Listen, if you want us to help you find them, one sniff of a sock or shoe and those dogs will be on the hunt, but…"

Fearing what the dogs would do if they did find Frank, the boys' mother nervously said, "no, no thank you sheriff," Lynn said. "Sorry to have bothered you, but we were worried that maybe the boys were hurt, but now that Adam's come home, we know better."

To be polite but hoping the men would say no, she continued and asked, "could I get you some coffee before you go?"

"No, but that's very nice of you. Good to see you, Mr. Cole. I know all the kids love your books," the sheriff said while reaching out to shake hands. "Sorry to hear you might be leaving soon what with the drilling and all. It's a shame really, a lot of the locals can't decide if they like the idea or not."

"I've decided I don't like it," Grandpa replied. "They have the farm, which was something I maybe did not fight enough to stop, but they will have a brawl on their hands if they think they will get the house."

"Well, good luck to you," and then the sheriff pointed down the road as if something could be seen. Everyone looked. "You know the Baker place started like this. The gas company bought up the surrounding land, put in these huge concrete slabs to drill from and I guess they will start testing soon."

"Now they're fighting in court to get Baker out. Folks like the money, but they don't like being told what to do. And those concrete slabs are as big as tennis courts. It's like they're getting prepped to launch rockets. What's a landowner supposed to do with those huge platforms left behind if the gas guys do lose and we run them out of town?"

"I suppose you could play tennis on them?" Mom said meekly.

The sheriff cocked his head to the side like a dog that had heard a strange sound, and then decided to ignore the comment. "You can't get near the Red Hook Diner or the hardware store without having to choose sides. The governor may be coming to town to have a town hall meeting." And then he straightened his posture a bit and stood tall. "I'll be there of course helping out with security."

The sheriff continued but leaned in towards Grandpa and spoke in a whisper. “Between you and me, rumor is the gas guys may be shifting gears, maybe drill on the other side of the river over near Woodstock. Who knows? You may get it all back, yet!”

“I hadn’t heard that sheriff. I do have the right to buy the place back if they back out. Who knows anything with them? That’s progress I guess.” Grandpa said to the sheriff while leading him to his car. “Why don’t you bring the family around next week? If I do have to pack, I’ve got too many books and if I have any that they haven’t read yet, I’d be happy to hand them out.”

“Well, that’s great, we might just do that,” then he turned to the boy’s father. “Listen, John, was it? Don’t be too hard on the boys. This is a mess, I agree, but boys will be boys. You know. I’m sure your oldest will pop up soon.”

Even thought he was the one who made the call, John now wanted the sheriff gone. Aware that the dogs were getting loud and excited, he said, “Not to worry, sheriff, I intend to place the whole blame on those little critters in the grass that Albert here filled your children’s heads with.”

“Hey, that’s the spirit! Well, I guess we’ll shove off now, have a nice day.” With that the sheriff turned towards the two men standing in the distance. Each of them had a dog on a leash.

One of the men spoke up and said, “hey sheriff, Boomer found a toy in the grass and got a scent. Shall I send him tracking?”

Lynn overheard what the man had said, and closed her eyes hoping the sheriff would put the dogs back in the truck.

In response to the dog handler, the sheriff turned back to the family, took another look at the barn, shuffled his hat back and forth in his hands, and then reached for the handle on his car.

"Nope, Boomer and his buddy will have to be heroes on another day." Then as he put on his hat and waved goodbye to the group, said, "let's leave these fine folks to take care of things. The boy'll be home by lunch, I reckon."

And with that the two cars started up and began down the drive.

The truck with the dogs in the back seat had the window down, and a huge tan colored dog – Lynn figured that would be Boomer, stuck his head out and howled. When the car turned around, the dog jumped to the other side and seemed to be concentrating on the front lawn. With its big ears flapping in the wind the car pulled out onto the main road and followed the blue and white police car back to town.

Mom hadn't noticed that she had stopped breathing and let out a sigh of relief.

"Had to call the cops on me, hey John, didn't believe me, did you?"

"Listen Dad, this morning I didn't know what to think. I called the moment this had all started, way before we had a chance to speak to Adam. Forget it, will you, just what do we do now?"

"I should be the one to apologize," Albert started to say. "I'm the one that filled Frank's head with the story. I should have thrown that darn sled out years ago. He never would have caught them without it."

As he spoke, John and Lynn made their way to the porch and sat together on the bench by the front door. Albert, the boys' grandfather, scanned the front yard for something he knew he could not see, and then turned to the lone tree in the distance, standing tall against the sky surrounded by an iron fence. Old Rusty seemed to be staring back, waving his arms laden with huge yellowish-brown apples.

Albert muttered to himself as if talking to the tree… '*I know, I know, I am aware.*'

TWELVE

Frank had been following his new friends through the grass, and noticed that every once in a while, they would come upon a small clearing in the grass and there would be a small pile of twigs, standing on end, leaning against each other in the shape of a small campfire. *'These must be the twigs used for the fires at night when they make their food coals,'* Frank thought to himself.

After following for a while, the Orchard Walker in front of Frank turned and spoke. "My name is Quartz. Keep following me. It is important that you step around and don't disturb these piles of twigs. We will cook them later for food coals."

"I thought that's what they were," said Frank. "I'll be careful. I think my grandpa would call you a Power Orchard Walker. I could tell by that blade of grass around your waist, or whatever the middle of you is called."

"Yes, I have certain powers, which we call gifts, given to us by the land we walk, and you may call us Orchard Walkers, but that was a name given to us by the older Notus."

Turning to his side and pointing, Quartz continued. "This is Ria," whom Frank could see was wearing a belt as well.

Then Quartz added, "We're almost there."

As far as Frank could tell, there was no difference between Quartz and Ria except that Quartz's body had a single point at the top that tilted slightly as he walked. Ria was also carrying a pack of twigs on her back, and the top of her head had two smaller points.

Ria's pack was similar to the one that Frank was wearing with the Meadow Twig in it. Ria had helped Frank take the safety pin off his back and left it in the grass. He now wore the pack with two straps that Ria and Quartz had quickly fashioned from fresh grass. It wasn't much different than the one he wore to school, except the one at home wasn't magical like this one.

As they stepped out into a small clearing of low grass, Frank saw a group of the Orchard Walkers in the distance discussing something. Just as Frank came closer into this larger clearing, he noticed that one Orchard Walker in the group didn't seem to be listening, but rather was staring straight at Frank. One by one, each of the other Walkers turned to look at the new visitor. Frank felt as if he were the smallest of the small in this small world that is the world of the Orchard Walker.

"Is that Edalb?" he whispered to Ria.

But before she could speak, the one who had been looking at him left the crowd and came forward. "Yes, I am the Edalb, Carrier of the Blade. Please turn and let me see the Meadow Twig in your pack. We have been waiting a long time for its return. The winds, rains, and roots had shown that the return of the twig would come in this cycle. The tunnels run deep, and the daily yawn is sufficient."

Frank had questions about what he had just heard, but he followed orders and turned his back to the group.

Edalb took a long look at the twig but did not touch it. "The clan is prepared; the cycle tells me that this warm year would be right. Notus sent you of course. How is he?"

Frank had been around the Orchard Walker stories as long as he could remember and even though the conversation was hard to believe, for some reason he was comfortable and wasn't as nervous as he thought he would be.

"You mean my grandfather," Frank explained. "I came, I mean my brother and I both came to see you without telling him. I dreamed about meeting a real Orchard Walker, and he told me the truth about you."

Edalb chuckled, "A dream? Do you often dream about journeys such as this? Tell me about this dream."

Frank decided not to tell about how he trapped one under a jar during the dream. "It was weird, I mean I caught an Orchard Walker, and he spoke to me. It was in rhyme, like a poem. Grandpa said you were speaking to me in my sleep."

"It may seem as much, but I could not speak to you while you sleep. But there are connections at play here between our world and that of the Notus. Small webs of cycle dust that mingle in our minds."

Edalb continued. "Did this Orchard Walker have a name? What was this "truth" that you found by dreaming this way?"

"Well," Frank began, feeling like now might be a good time to get nervous. "Before the dream, I thought you weren't real. I mean I thought the stories, your story, was fiction."

"So, if we were not real, something you call fiction. Why did you come to find us? What did you hope to gain?"

Frank wasn't sure how much to say about his grandfather, but he went on. "After the dream, I shared it with Grandpa, and to him, it seemed like you were sending a message to him, through me. So, he told me about when he was here, or somewhere with the Orchard Walkers."

Frank continued. “I’m not sure what you mean by me ‘gaining’ something. I’m trying to help.” And then he turned his back again. “Take the pack and I’ll go home.”

Seeing how Edalb seemed to be ignoring him, Frank turned back to the clan leader and hoping he wasn’t giving away secrets he would later regret, he said, “He didn’t tell me much, and I wasn’t sure if I should believe him or not, but then my brother and I saw you last night, from our window. The lights in the grass.

Edalb seemed to be nodding his head when he spoke. “Webs of cycle dust.”

“Huh?” Frank wasn’t sure he had heard correctly, but Edalb was still ignoring him.

Then Edalb moved forward and turned his head side to side. “All in good time, young notus, what brought you here and what controls what happens next will all be revealed. I will only admit that I know too much to question them, these webs that spread before us in time. I have seen the webs of cycle dust move nature in ways a notus would never believe… could never believe. What you call fiction is perhaps more real, than even you are.

Now the small crowd had seemed to grow to a large number of Orchard Walkers. Each of them seemed to twinkle from one shade of green to another. It was difficult for Frank to see their outlines as they all merged into a curtain of grass blades. Edalb continued, but was now speaking to all of them, and not just Frank.

"We cannot control, nor would change the way a tree extends a leaf, a blossom, then a bud, then sweet fruit, only to then sleep a full cycle."

Frank almost jumped when Edalb turned quickly and said, "Each cycle of life, my young notus, whether it be a warm cycle or cold, each has a web that connects them, and the dust that moves from one cycle to the next cycle through the web is just the start of the mystery that most ignore each day. And so, it shall be. If we are here, there, or nowhere, the cycle goes on, the web stays connected, and the dust moves like pollen on the tail of a bee. It flickers in the starlight like dust, and like the dreams you dream, floats to where it must."

And as if to make a point directly to Frank, he leaned in towards the young boy sweeping his hand around the circle of creatures. "And the dust that made us, is the same that makes you. Did I send you a message in your sleep, or did your sleep connect you to your grandfather's dream?

"This earth is ours, notus, both yours and mine. The winds make that known. We appear to you as leaves of common grass, but the winds push us both in equal ways. You will see. You will see. All in good time. All in good time."

Frank didn't know what to think, or really what Edalb was talking about, but said, "I'm not sure what all that means, all I know is Grandpa, uh… I mean Notus will be glad, I think, that I came here. My brother went back and told them I found you so I'm sure they know where I am by now. Like I said, they didn't know that I was coming."

Thinking it might be a good time to say goodbye, Frank turned his back on Edalb and pointed to the small backpack again and said. "Now if you can take this thing off my back I'll go home and tell Grandpa that everything is okay."

Edalb's mouth formed a perfect circle when he said, "Oh, you must know that you cannot leave the twig with me. An Orchard Walker cannot return the twig to the root of the Deep Tree. Only a Notus like yourself can put the Meadow Twig back, as it was a Notus, your grandfather, which took it out. You must and will come with us to the Deep Tree. We are prepared for the journey."

Edalb continued, "Was it as simple as me to put back the Meadow Twig I would have done it many years ago. Daily for two warm years Notus placed the Meadow Twig on the edge of the grasses. For over three hundred nights we could only stare and not touch. It would have been no use for us to try. In those years, the clan grew, but we suffered as well."

Edalb began to pace and raised his voice. "We knew the order of the twig and could not challenge it. If we even took it for a moment, your grandfather would have thought us complete and safe, and we would have been far from safe. So no, we kept the twig company each day but let it be. Each night Notus came and took it back. The pain on his face matched ours. To this day he carries the guilt of our fate."

This Frank understood completely. "I know," said Frank sadly.

Taking a seat in the circle of bare ground, Edalb asked, "what does one so young know?" Edalb asked.

"I've been thinking about how happy my grandfather was when I told him about the dream." And Frank could see Edalb nodding. "He must think I am the answer, like I'm supposed to be here."

Edalb brought both hands together and said, "It isn't a think we think, young Notus, it is a thing he and I both know. You are the answer. You are to deliver the twig not to me, no, no, not to me, but to the base of the Deep Tree, and then your grandfather will see you home and safe, fulfilling the dream, fulfilling his dream. With the twig in place, your grandfather will be at peace, and so will our place in the world be restored."

Looking around at the growing crowd, Edalb said, "We have been lost for too long. Lost, and only able to watch as the Deep Tree moved from cycle to cycle, and I fear getting weaker. It needs us, as much as we need it."

Edalb brightened when Frank said, "Is that the web you were talking about?"

"Frank," Edalb said, agreeing. "We need you for this, it is important. It is beyond your age to understand, and yet... Notus will understand and Notus will be grateful." And then, as if to make sure Frank was listening, Edalb spread his arms out and gave the slightest bow, and said, "Edalb will be grateful."

And then Edalb turned and walked away leaving Frank with Quartz and Ria, surrounded by all the others.

'Wow,' thought Frank as he looked around. *'There are so many more of them now.'*

Frank couldn't make out much of what was being said, but the murmurs were loud. He heard some talking amongst themselves about his grandfather. He heard some talk about the 'old notus' and the 'young notus.'

"Quartz?" Frank asked. How long will it take to get to the Deep Tree so that I can go home?"

Quartz turned to Ria who said, “The trip to the Deep Tree will take two days.” She then added, “You should know, the Edalb regards you with high honor even if you do not see it. You are now a part of the cycle. Breaking it now would be a loss that cannot be measured against anything but time. All would suffer.”

‘How did she know I was thinking about ditching?’ Frank thought. *‘If I really just dropped this twig and took off this necklace and ran home what could happen?’*

But when he thought about what Edalb said, and about his grandfather spending so much time trying to get this twig back, he realized he had to go through with it.

Frank heard Ria call Edalb, ‘The Edalb’ and wondered what she meant. *‘Was Edalb his name, or was it a title, like ‘King’?’*

He decided to ask about that later, and instead spoke to Ria. “I’m not sure about all this, but I think my grandfather would understand if I went with you. And my dad did say that maybe I could camp out on this trip to the farm.”

Finally sure that he was ready for the task ahead, Frank straightened his shoulders, stood tall, and said, “Okay, I’ll go with you, but I can’t stay too long, when do you think we can leave?”

Edalb heard Frank even from across the way and called out, “Tonight, young Notus, tonight when the food coal fires are out! Tonight, as the moon replaces the sun, as the butterflies rest, before the firefly flies. In less than many days we will see you set the twig Notus. Set the twig and settle the Orchard Walkers back on the middle meadow. Now that you are with us, the Branch Bridge will rise once more before the warm year gets covered by the cold."

Frank didn't know how to respond. He was worried but had faith in the stories he knew that his grandfather had shared. *'I'll go,'* he said to himself, *'Nothing in Grandpa's books ever mentioned anything to worry about. They're just kid books.'*

Frank was full of questions and was getting a little more relaxed, even though the number of Orchard Walkers around him had swelled to a huge crowd. "Where is this Middle Meadow?" he asked. "And what makes it so special?"

The Orchard Walkers who were in the clearing, came around to look at their new friend. All of them seemed impressed by the Meadow Twig. One spoke up and said, "Most of us have never been to the Middle Meadow or seen the Meadow Twig."

Now Frank saw how they all started nodding and mumbling. '*Oh my gosh,'* Frank thought, *'Not only have they never seen a human before, but they've also never seen their home either! I have to help them.'*

Frank had not seen Quartz come up behind him and was startled when he whispered in his ear. Quartz looked different. *'Was Quartz getting taller?' Frank wondered. 'Am I getting smaller?'*

"I'm glad you're with us Frank, we will help you see it through. The cycle is strong, and so are you." Hearing this from his new friend made Frank even more positive about the decision he made this morning.

Frank followed Quartz and was taken to a small gathering where preparations were being made for the journey. "Rest here, Notus. You will tire of the twists and turns we are required to make in order to move with the web of roots. As we move underground, the obstacles seemed to be put there on purpose to slow us down."

"The distance is not so great, as you can see," Quartz said pointing to the big tree in the distance. "But no roots grow in straight lines and the spring water will require navigation. Under these conditions, even small distances become more like an epic journey."

"Quartz, how did you get here?" Frank asked. "I mean, where do you come from? Are there Orchard Walkers all over the world?"

"According to the Edalb, there are others. We have been away so long we do not know how many are still waiting for us on the meadow." Quartz began. "Once the clan was in a long thin canyon between two mountains. It was before my time, but I learned that one day a great shadow came over the land and the earth began to shake. Then out of nowhere a river came and filled the canyon. The clan barely made it out. Trees were falling down all around them. They were almost trapped."

"So how did they get out?" Frank asked. "Did they use the trees and float out?"

Quartz pondered the idea of floating on a tree and shook his head violently back and forth. "Oh no, we would never float on a tree," and Frank thought he saw him shudder. "With the power of his sword Edalb was able to cut through the trees and lead the clan up the canyon wall with the rising water chasing them. Once they got over the crest of the canyon, the water rose no more, and they were safe. To be sure the water would not surprise them again, they headed to the mountains."

"All of the underground root ways were flooded so Edalb led the clan over the mountains to a new place not far from here, where they eventually found a new path to the Middle Meadow. During the journey over the hills is when we saw this place, and eventually we came back to make it part of our home. That is when we met your grandfather."

The twig attached to Frank's back was getting uncomfortable, and he shifted in his seat. "Tell me about the Middle Meadow. Have you been there?"

Quartz laughed, "Oh no, no one has been there since Notus had the twig. It will be wonderful when we return. Legend says the Middle Meadow floats in the eddy of the stream created by the Branch Bridge. The Branch Bridge is our 'door' to the meadow. The meadow is huge, and it has many, many bridges that connect to it. Each bridge leading to another home of sub-walkers. We are completely safe there and have access to many lands."

"What's an eddy, wait, what do you mean by sub-walker?" Frank asked.

"An eddy is like a still spot in the river. You must have dropped a twig in the river and seen how the water moves around it, but at times, the twig remains still in the moving water, and doesn't float downstream? That is an eddy.

"And sub-walker?" Frank pressed the question.

"Notus, your grandfather gave us the name Orchard Walker. We are subterranean creatures who walk on two feet, so we call ourselves sub-walkers. We spend more than half of our lives underground, so subterranean, which means 'under the earth.' There are many of us in many clans. I suppose you could call them a name by where they live, such as dessert walker or forest walker. We like it here in the orchard, so we like the name Orchard Walker."

Before Frank could ask Quartz why he seemed to be getting taller, Quartz stopped him and said, "And now I have to prepare for our journey. My only hope is to get there without running into the Enots, it's about-"

But Quartz was interrupted by Edalb coming through the blades of grass.

Frank jumped up. "Edalb, Quartz was telling me about the Meadow. But I have a question… I mean questions."

Now Edalb looked from Quartz to Frank. "What is it young Notus?"

"I never heard of the Enots," Frank said, becoming a little worried. "Are these Enots anything we should be afraid of? Do they still live around here?"

"Oh yes," Edalb said. "The Enots… not to worry, not to worry. The Enots are still around, but the Enots, you see, are small in number, and stay away from us. I do not think you have to worry about them. They fear the Edalb, I am certain."

"But will we know if they are following us? Do they want to stop us from getting to the Middle Meadow?"

"No, no, no, no, no." said Edalb. "The actually would like to be on the meadow with us. Let them try, though we will do our best to avoid them, you'll see. You'll see and learn while we travel among the roots. They are banished, we will stay ahead. Not to worry."

Despite Frank feeling certain that he was safe with the Orchard Walkers, the more Edalb said *not to* worry Frank began to worry more about the Enots. *'I wonder why Grandpa never mentioned this to me?'* he thought.

Before Frank could ask about how he seemed to be shrinking, Edalb and the others ignored Frank as they prepared for the journey.

THIRTEEN

Adam woke up later that day and gave the three grownups the whole story from beginning to end. He didn't leave out anything and felt good about the fact that he didn't blame Frank for it but told his mom and dad that it was both of their ideas. Adam could tell that his parents were upset with Grandpa, even though they didn't say anything out loud. Adam could tell by the way his dad kept looking over at Grandpa while they listened to his story.

Grandpa kept telling them not to worry. "Edalb will take care of Frank, I'm as sure of that as I'm standing here. He'll be back today, or tomorrow the latest."

"Tomorrow! I need to see him today, not tomorrow." But Mom realized there was nothing that could be done about it. As she turned to look out the window at the orchard, she said, "I don't like the idea of Frank spending the night out."

"Well, we're not going to sit around all day," said Dad. "We can at least continue to look for him. There are still spots I can think of that I may have gone by too quickly this morning."

And so, they did. Even Adam joined them as they all spent the remainder of the day looking for Frank by the edge of the lawn where the grass and hay field meet. While Adam was crawling around, he found an old bottle cap and a safety pin just like the one Frank was wearing but there was no sign of The Orchard Walkers or his brother anywhere.

Adam had mixed feelings about the search and was thinking, *'I'd like to know that he's okay, but I really want him to help Edalb.'* Then he leaned down and whispered into the grass, “Good luck, Frank.” But he knew or guessed that no one was listening.

Feeling like it was hopeless to continue the search, they all stayed in after dinner. Adam went up to his room. The more he thought about his brother, he got more and more worried about Frank staying out overnight, and yet, he wished that he could be there with him. He propped his pillow against the wall and sat up in bed watching the sun disappear into the hills. When the sun set behind Old Rusty it gave the appearance of a huge hand reaching out of the ground. The spooky image made Adam turn away from the window.

Downstairs Dad again mentioned that maybe they should call back the guy with the dogs, but mom got upset thinking about strangers running around stomping on the grass. “I don’t want him out there anymore than you do, but what can we do? I’m going to go out with a flashlight once it gets dark, but if that doesn’t work, I think we need to give it a day. I’m willing to give it a day.”

Grandpa seemed calm and sure that Frank was okay. Twice he said something about Adam being the proof that Frank was ‘at least somewhere in the orchard’ and sleeping out with the Orchard Walkers. “We know *where* he is, we just don’t know exactly where he is.” He exclaimed while washing the dishes after dinner.

After a while Dad came up to put Adam to bed. He tucked Adam’s covers in real tight and then sat down on the bed. After a minute or so Adam peeked up at his father thinking he had left the room but saw that he was looking out the window. The moon was full, and it was bright outside. Adam felt like he should say sorry or something, but instead closed his eyes just in time before his dad turned and kissed him goodnight. From where Adam lay, he was able to see his father turn out the light in the room and walk down the hall and cross to Grandpa's writing room.

As the boys' father entered the room, he sat on the old rocker and started looking at the books that were piled on the shelf next to the chair. *'Maybe there's a clue in here where we can find Frank and put an end to this,'* he said to himself. After reading several children's books, all of which he had read before, he tossed the last one on a small pile of papers.

"They're all the same, just kid stories." He said aloud. Then he admitted to himself, *'I guess I've read each of these over the years at least a dozen times.'*

He leaned back in his chair to think about what he should do next when he noticed a small leather book on the top shelf, lying on its side. "Say, what's this?"

Checking first down the hall to be sure he was alone, he got up and took the book off the shelf. It looked like a diary. It was handwritten and very old. At first Dad thought it might be private and decided to leave it alone, but when he flipped the book to the first page, he noticed that someone had written a title there. It was in pencil, as if a child had written it. It simply said "Edalb."

Upon seeing the title, he sat back down and flipped the pages through his fingers. It didn't look like more than twenty pages or so had any writing on them, so he settled in and began to read them. After only a few pages, he realized that the book must have been written by Albert when he was a boy. It was, he realized, the original story of what happened to Albert when he was first taken in by the Orchard Walkers just about sixty years ago.

Downstairs, Mom, and the boys' grandfather were having coffee after another unsuccessful search of the lawn. Mom was pacing back and forth in front of the kitchen table. "Dad, how can we be sure that Frank is okay, maybe things have changed since you were a boy," she said.

"I'm sure everything is fine. Best as I can tell, the Orchard Walkers haven't changed in hundreds of years, and these fellas have been right here, on this lawn for the last sixty." As he spoke, he looked out the window, over the sink. "Oh, look at this Lynn, they're off, it's happening. They're going back home to the Middle Meadow."

He moved aside a little to make room for his daughter, and continued, "That's proof that Frank is still with them, and everything is okay. It won't be long now, you'll see!"

Albert's daughter had not realized the impact this was having on her father until she saw him brush away a tear. All of her heart wanted her little boy back, but a small piece of her wanted her son to succeed in seeing the Orchard Walkers back to their home.

With a mix of excitement and worry, she ran to the porch door. In the distance out on the lawn was a string of little lights in the grass. The line ran from the center of the lawn out to the edge of the woods. It wasn't a straight line but seemed to be in a zigzag pattern. "It's moving!" She declared, but then Mom had another thought. "Dad, how will Frank get home, let's follow them!"

"We can't follow them; you would never catch them. We were just out there and saw nothing. They're too good at hiding." Then Grandpa pointed to the woods. "See how the lights go out when they reach the woods? It would be a wild goose chase, believe me, I've tried for years to contact them. It just can't be done. I mean they have no use for us now and would never let us near."

Walking away from the window, Albert clasped his hands together and shook them. Turning back to his daughter, he said, "This is an excellent sign. Frank will get home safe; they'll see to that."

Lynn turned toward the front steps to call for John, to tell him what was happening, but she saw now that he had been standing in the doorway listening. In his hand he was holding a small book, his thumb resting on a page holding it open. Lynn smiled and told him the good news, but he ignored it and faced his father-in-law with a scowl on his face.

He did not seem happy with what Lynn told him.

"Honey," she said. "What's wrong?"

Ignoring his wife, he turned to her father and said, "Albert, tell me you made up the part about the Enots."

At first the old man looked at John with a puzzled look then saw that John was holding his old journal. Upon seeing it, he closed his eyes and rubbed his forehead.

"Oh, my goodness," then he turned to look back out the door. "How in the world could I have forgotten about the Enots?"

Mom saw the worried look on the two men and yelled, "Will someone please tell me what the heck an Enot is?" But neither man answered. "Give me that book!" she said.

The worry that was starting to go away had just come back to her.

It only took a minute for her to read the page that her husband showed her. “Dad, is this true about the Enots, that they almost hurt you? Why did you keep this a secret?”

Grandpa came back and sat at the table. He was rubbing the side of his face; it looked like he was trying to think of something. “Yes, it’s all true, I wrote that all down-”

Interrupting, Dad slammed his hand down on the table, “Frank could be in real danger, how could you forget?”

Despite being upset, Albert tried to explain. “When I young, my fifth-grade teacher, Mrs. Shea, gave me special permission to spend my recess time writing my story. Of course, she thought it was complete fiction. She had no clue that I was writing the story of my days with the Orchard Walkers.”

“I won a school-wide writing award with that story, and later, when I got older, and you had children, I thought to write a children’s book. I wrote it for your children, for everyone’s children.”

I wanted the story of the Orchard Walkers to be loved by kids. I never wanted to include any violence or bad things, so I left that part out; the part that included the Enots. Later, when the story became popular, I just kept the Orchard Walkers living in a perfect world and never thought to include the Enots.”

Grandpa turned and looked away as if in deep thought. “Since I never included them in any of my stories, I just forgot about them over the years, and never even told the boys. Believe me, the last thing on my mind was that they would someday be able to catch an Orchard Walker and go and be with them. It wasn’t supposed to ever happen this way.”

Seemingly in deep thought, the old man took a seat at the kitchen table.

Adam wasn't able to sleep and had come down after his father for a glass of water. He had been listening on the back stairs, by the pantry door. He startled everyone when he spoke up.

"We have to go get Frank, Grandpa, I did it once, I know I can do it again. I feel better now."

Startled, grandpa got up and went over to Adam, looked down at the brave boy and smiled, trying not to let his grandson get frightened. "Adam, they're gone little buddy. Besides, I think they were waiting for you today. It was a one in a million shot that you caught them."

He then added, "Besides, they have the Meadow Twig now. They don't need you, or me, anymore."

Mom asked the question that was on everyone's mind. "Dad, Frank will be safe with the Orchard Walkers, won't he? I mean, they won't hurt him?"

Grandpa tried to make everyone feel better about things. "Listen," he said, "they need Frank to put in the Meadow Twig. They won't hurt him. If they can get to the meadow, and the bridge is exposed, Frank will be a hero." And then he remembered Adam was listening, and said, "He and Adam, too, will be famous and friends forever to the Orchard Walker clan."

"Don't worry about him, they need him and will protect him above all else!"

"But" said Dad, "do the Enots know how much the Orchard Walkers need Frank?"

“I don’t know… I don’t think so…” Grandpa answered then turned toward the screen door that led to the porch. “I just don’t know.”

In a moment, the old man was on the porch looking out over the lawn, watching as the lights slowly went away, disappearing into the woods.

Then, as if the fading lights could hear him, Grandpa whispered, “Edalb, a long time ago I saved your life... now return the favor and bring me back my grandson.”

FOURTEEN

After waiting out the day, prepping in the lawn in front of the house, the Orchard Walkers were set to move once the sun went down. As best as Frank could see, fifty or sixty of the Orchard Walkers made up the march holding torches. Other Orchard Walkers carrying packs or what looked like tools, stood in between the torch carriers.

Once they started out, Edalb and Frank walked behind Quartz, who had his own torch and seemed to be leading everyone. Frank wondered what the torches would look like from his bedroom window. Such small sticks with a little flame on top that never seemed to actually burn any of the wood. Frank had roasted enough marshmallows on sticks to know that either the sticks or the fire was not normal.

At first, Frank had a lot of trouble getting through the grass, but then realized it would get easier if he followed the exact path of Edalb, who in turn, was following the path made by Quartz. Rather than take a straight path to the woods, it looked like the line went back and forth from one coal fire to the next, picking up even more Orchard Walkers along the way.

"How did you get to be the leader, Edalb? Is it because you're the oldest?" Before waiting for an answer, he went on. "And are you getting bigger or am I getting smaller? I feel like something is going on." It was just a few of hundreds of questions Frank had on his mind.

Edalb turned slightly, keeping up the pace of walking through the grass. "Let me ease your mind. You are NOT getting smaller. Let me correct that. Of course, since you are alive, you are growing each day, but yes, all the members of the clan are growing faster, which you may have noticed."

"As walkers, we are all part of the natural world, so like you, we all do grow slightly each day, but you may have noticed that we are slightly taller than we were at the start of the day. It is one of the reasons we prefer to come out at night and stay underground during the day."

Now Edalb turned his back to Frank but continued to walk and talk. "To an orchard, the sun gives the trees nourishment, as it does to all things that surround it, and to the apples in the orchard, the sun helps them color, but to a subterranean walker, it magnifies our natural growth speeding up the process. There are tricks to staying small and if we need to hide, we have our methods. Normally we would have gone underground early, but we were prepping for our journey and the change is only slight in one day. It will reverse once we go under."

"To your other question, let me just say this. It is true, I am the oldest Orchard Walker in the clan, but that is not why I am the leader. It is because I have the true power of the blade, given to me by the blade itself. You can see that others carry blades as well, and many Orchard Walkers have developed and you may even say perfected the power of their tool, but mine is a gift greater than all others combined."

Stopping so quickly, Frank nearly bumped into him, Edalb continued. "But in part, I am only the oldest of course because of your grandfather, the great Notus, who once saved my life. If it were not for him, I would have no age at all, existing only in the dust."

Now Frank couldn't contain himself. "He saved your life? How? He was just a kid like me, wasn't he? When did this happen?"

“All in good time, young Notus, all in good time.” Then Edalb grabbed something from what looked like a pile of stones on the ground and tossed it to Frank. “In the meantime, eat something, the journey will be long.”

Frank thought Edalb had thrown a small rock to him, and he almost dropped it when it landed so lightly in his hand. “What is this? Is this a food coal?”

Frank liked when Edalb called him the young Notus and liked using their words for things. He never thought that by reading his grandfather’s books he would learn a new language, but now he used the words of the Orchard Walkers like he was one of them. It made him feel like a part of the clan.

The response came from behind him as the other coals were being gathered and handed back through the line. “Yes... food coals, try it, it will give you strength.”

Frank had forgotten how hungry he was, so even though this ‘food’ seemed kind of gross, he made himself ready. He smelled the thing first. It had no odor at all, and even though Frank knew it was made from special twigs that were burned in the fires, it didn’t leave any marks in his hand like the burnt sticks that he used sometimes around a campfire. *‘Besides,’* thought Frank, *‘I’m starving.’* Then he broke off a piece and chewed it a little.’

“Hey, this isn’t bad! It feels like an apple in my mouth, but tastes a little like root beer, only not so sweet.”

“I know,” said Edalb.

“How do you know what root beer tastes like?” *‘Maybe he just knows everything,’* thought Frank.

"I don't know what root beer tastes like, but your grandfather said the exact same thing one hundred and twenty years ago."

"You can't mean that... Grandpa isn't over a hundred years old."

"You forget," Edalb said to him as he held back a blade of grass for Frank to walk through. "You see to us, it was a hundred and twenty years ago, but for you, only sixty. What you call autumn and winter, is one cold year for us, what you call spring and summer, we call one warm year. Every one year for you, gives us two… one warm and one cold.

"So, to your grandfather it was only sixty years ago I ran over the Branch Bridge, stumbled, and was pulled from beneath the rapid river, by your grandfather, our Notus friend. I thought you knew about that."

"Darn it, I forgot about The Orchard Walkers having half years. So that's how the great um, I mean my grandfather saved your life? You were drowning?"

Edalb didn't seem to be listening, so Frank continued, "You know we kind of have two years in a year, too. First. we have the warm year, then we have the school year, or at least that's what we call-"

"STOP!" Edalb turned and put one hand in front of Frank's face, and with the other hand pulled the blade from around his waist. Frank froze.

As the blade slid out from around the waist of their leader it seemed to get darker. Though still green, as Edalb pulled it away from his body, it seemed to go from a soft piece of grass to hardened steel. As it became the blade, Frank thought he heard a 'ringing sound' as the blade quivered in the air.

Edalb swung the blade over Frank's head in a circle, and even though the blade was well above his head, Frank instinctively ducked.

He heard the blade swoosh and quiver in the air and then he heard Edalb give a command, "BLADE… RETURN!"

Having made the order, Edalb released the blade over Frank's head back toward the parade of Orchard Walkers behind him. As it spun through the air, the sharp edge of the blade nicked and cut the torches ends off and put out each flame one by one as it sailed through the entire line of walkers. When it reached the end of the line, the blade silently turned midflight and returned back into the hands of Edalb, who caught it with one hand, just over Frank's head.

With one last circular motion, Edalb snuffed out the flame that Quartz was carrying then in the same motion, slid the blade around his waist, where it turned back into what looked like a simple blade of grass.

Frank was back on his feet, looking at Edalb as if he had just seen the best magic trick of his life. "Oh my gosh! What! Didja see that? Man, how did you-"

But before he could finish talking, Edalb grabbed the boy by the shoulder and told him to be quiet. "You must listen; Enots are nearby, stand close behind me. Put your back against my back. Make no noise."

Startled by Edalb's strength, and suddenly afraid, Frank did as he was told. Thinking Edalb was going to let Frank hide behind him, Frank moved in real close and got right behind him and closed his eyes. Edalb, needing to be sure the boy wasn't seen by the Enots, curled his body backwards, and rolled up like a blade of grass, with the Frank inside. The rest of the clan had already moved slowly together, curled into round blade-like grasses, shifted into a variety of grassy colors, and became camouflaged within the other grasses.

Frank thought he heard something moving toward him through the grass and took a chance and opened his eyes. When he realized that it was completely dark and he couldn't see, he moved a little wondering what was blocking his view.

"No, Notus," Edalb whispered, "Do not move a muscle, let them pass."

In about two minutes, Edalb went back to his regular form and let the boy out, "It's safe now, they have gone."

"Was it the Enots? I didn't know what to do! Thanks for hiding me. I didn't know you could do that."

"And I, young one, did not know how brave a Notus you were." Then he put his baseball mitt hand on Frank's shoulder. "I was concerned you would call out or make a noise."

"Maybe my mouth was stuck… I don't know if I was brave or scared," Frank said. He did not tell the old Orchard Walker that he thought he was more scared than brave.

"As we are all part of nature, our instinct moves us from fear to bravery. It's how most things survive. You are not here by accident, and you are prepared for what is to come. That the Enots are on the move has meaning as well. All are connected to the web that moves us all. We will have to move more silently now. There will be time to talk, time to talk, later.

The entire clan rested in order to give the Enots enough time to get farther away, and after he thought things were clear, Frank asked if there were a lot of Enots. Edalb told Frank that no, there were not so many, but they must be avoided at all costs. When Frank asked Quartz what the Enots looked like, the question was ignored. Frank thought that was weird and thought to himself, *'how am I supposed to avoid them if I don't even know what they look like?'*

While they rested, Edalb told Frank how, after the Orchard Walkers had made their way up the mountain during the flood, they found themselves in a rocky place without many trees. Edalb told him, "With few trees, we had few twigs. With few twigs… not much food!"

"We were doing our best to keep everyone fed, when we saw that finally the water was going down. Once we saw that we would soon be able to get back to our home, we sent small groups out to follow different paths in order to find out which way down the mountain would get us to the forest faster. That was when we discovered that the last packs of food had been replaced with stones."

Even though they never found out who took the food, Edalb explained how the Orchard Walkers gave the thieves the name Enots, which was 'stone' spelled backwards.

Edalb said, "We were desperate and with small remains of food coals. Mostly dust! We will never forgive the Enots, not ever."

After Edalb explained how the Enots had basically left them to die, Frank stopped thinking about the Enots as strange creatures, and realized, maybe, that the Enots were another bunch of Orchard Walkers, or at least a particular kind of sub-walker.

He thought, *'maybe they're not scary looking, but what would they think about me helping Edalb?'* Frank decided to stick with Quartz, Ria, and the rest of this clan, and not wander too far. He thought about the pack on his back and what the Enots might do to get it from him.

Edalb must have been reading Frank's mind, when he said. "Stay close, Notus. We will bring the Meadow Twig to its rightful place."

"My grandfather told me he went with you to the Middle Meadow."

"Oh yes, but that was many, many, years later. But such a good thing he was with us."

"Tell me how he saved you from the river." Frank wanted to know everything.

"All in good time, Notus, all in good time."

"What about this cycle you keep talking about, what is -?"

But he was interrupted by Edalb. "You, young one, have too many questions, and we have a distance to go." Edalb got up, and so did the many other Orchard Walkers. "We will talk again when we rest again. For now, we will find a root that will show us the way. Ria will take the lead tonight. But no more torches, and no more talking, the Enots may be close by."

Once Ria went ahead, the only light was from the half-moon that seemed to be smiling down on the clan. Frank's eyes grew accustomed to the darkness, and after only one food coal and a little water, he felt like he had taken a long nap, and eaten a huge meal.

He made up his mind that he trusted Edalb and walked right behind he and Quartz as they quietly made their way through the woods.

FIFTEEN

After assuring Adam that Frank would be okay, even though the three grownups did have some worries of their own, Adam finally went back to bed. Mom and Dad went out onto the porch where Grandpa was sitting. The lights in the lawn were gone now. The only lights came from the stars in the sky, and the small reflection of the moon, which seemed to be cut in half, like a slanted smile in the sky.

Looking at the moon, mom pointed to it and said, "that's the only thing smiling tonight."

It was true though. The reflection on the moon was strong and lit up the apple trees whose shadows seemed shaped like soldiers in the field. In the distance, they could all see the huge tree on the hill, Old Rusty, silhouetted in the distance.

Just below Old Rusty there was a small spring of water that came from the ground and ran through the weeds creating a series of small fresh-water pools. That water, along with a number of other springs further up in the hills, eventually joined to become one small stream that poured into the brook that ran by the barn.

Grandpa noticed his daughter and son-in-law gazing off into the distance. "Have you ever noticed that before? It only happens when the moon is at a certain height." he said. "I mean how the water seems to come directly from below Old Rusty?"

Dad had never seen it before, and even though he was thinking of his son wandering around in the dark, he still thought it was amazing how the light seemed to highlight the tree and what looked like a small fountain coming out of the ground.

Mom interrupted his thought when she said, "Yes, I know it doesn't happen very often, but I've seen it a few times." Then she added, "I used to think it was beautiful, but now it looks to me like the tree is crying, like I am."

Mom saying what she said brought Dad back to his son. "Albert, did you remember anything else about the Enots. The book doesn't say what they look like."

"I never saw one to find out! They were never around the meadow where I was. I got the sense that the Enots did not know where the meadow was!"

"There was a bridge to the Meadow; it was controlled by the Meadow Twig. It's like a key. Without having the key, I guess the Enots stayed off the Meadow, and the Orchard Walkers never let them on. If they knew for all these years that I had the twig, well, I guess they weren't much of a problem. Now that the Orchard Walkers are on their way back, I don't know if the Enots know or not."

"You never saw one?" asked Mom, now slightly relieved. "If you never saw one, maybe they won't bother Frank either."

Albert turned and looked at his daughter and smiled. He decided not to tell her that the reason he never saw one was because he had been running away from the Enots so fast, he never got a good look at one.

He remembered his last day on the Middle Meadow. He would have left the day before, but when Edalb tripped on the Branch Bridge and went into the water, the leader of the clan gave Albert one more night as a reward for pulling him out of the rapids. That day Albert went off the meadow with a group of Orchard Walkers collecting wood to be used in the coal fires and for making tools. The activity was called ‘twigging,’ and Albert was excited about going. Since Albert had become such a curiosity, almost all of the Orchard Walker clan decided to come with him.

When they all got over the Branch Bridge, Albert pulled the Meadow Twig out of a place in a tree root that looked like a wooden knot. Taking the twig out of the root lowered the bridge back into the water locking out anyone from getting on the meadow. Albert had seen it done by others and did not think it was that big of a deal who pulled it out, but Edalb wasn’t happy that Albert pulled it out, and told him to put it right back.

Startled by Edalb’s shout, Albert turned to put the twig back but dropped it just as someone yelled that the Enots were approaching. Hearing something coming through the grass, and having learned to be afraid of the Enots, Albert guessed that they wanted the twig. Being afraid, and just a little boy, he grabbed the twig and ran.

Surprised that the boy had the twig, the Enots chased him. Frank was faster and dashed into one of the several tunnels among the underground roots. Not knowing which tunnel would take him to safety, he ran blindly but luckily found one that took him out from underground and into the woods.

As he exited the tunnel, the bright sunlight made it impossible to see the low branches of a nearby tree. After feeling the branches hit his face, he stumbled and fell to the ground. The same branch must have pulled the necklace from around his head as he fell. When he got up, he was full size and had the Meadow Twig in his hand.

He never did get to look at a real Enot.

Realizing his daughter was looking at him strangely, he shook off the daydream and simply said. “I’m sure all will be well. I was there for three days and never worried about any danger.”

The boy’s father now spoke up. “I heard what you said on the porch earlier. How did you save this Edalb’s life? What were you… twelve years old?”

“It was easy, John. And it happened so quickly. Yes, I was just twelve. While going out over the Branch Bridge from the Meadow, Edalb fell off into the water. There was always a breeze by the water, and I recall it being particularly windy at that moment. These guys are basically made of the same material as leaves or grass or whatever, and they’re very light.”

“Anyway, he fell and was being swept away down the river, and I swam in our river all the time, so I jumped in after him. I didn’t think anything of it. For a minute, I had forgotten I was small, but when I jumped into this little spring of water, it was like a river to me. Everyone else just stood there.”

“I found out later that they float forever but can’t swim. Anyway, I caught up to him and dragged him out. To the Orchard Walkers it was a really big deal. I don’t think he would have drowned, but he may have been lost in the river and never found. I’m not sure, actually.”

“Anyway, after we got out, I remember Edalb telling the clan that I was now part of the cycle. They let me spend another night with them because of it.”

“The cycle?” Both Lynn and John asked at the same time.

The old man continued, “As I can figure, the cycle is kind of like a spirit that guides them. Everything that happens in their lives, they believe, is all part of a big cycle of small events over time. I remember them talking about a web, how everything in nature, including you and I, are connected by this web affecting everything else. You might call it fate, or just think of it as what we call Mother Nature."

"Anyway, Edalb told the Orchard Walkers that my being there to save his life was part of this 'cycle' even before I got there, I was really too young to understand the whole thing. I tried when I got back, to write down as much as I could. That's the book you found, John."

"I wonder what Edalb has to say about the cycle now, after you ended up with the key to the meadow," said the boy's dad.

"What do you mean, John?

"By you taking the twig I mean, and them being stuck on your lawn for the last sixty years, instead of being home where they belong. I mean, if they honestly believe that our actions and theirs are connected by this *'web,'* then they would have to think that one day Frank would come to them and bring them back home."

"That was an accident, and really all my fault. It was wrong of me to even take the twig out of the tree. I was just a child. I tried for years to give it back to them, but never could. For two years straight, I put the twig down by the lawn before I went to bed, and then picked it up again in the morning."

"Eventually I got too old and tired of trying."

Dad had been thinking. "Listen, I don't like it, but I've seen enough today to believe in these walkers. I don't like that my son is walking with them, but if it's true that they sat out here for sixty years… think about that. They sat out here for sixty years waiting for magic. Waiting for Frank to have a dream and do what he did. I don't know where I'm going with this, but it means something. I'm just not sure what."

Both Mom and Albert stared at John, not exactly sure if there was more to what he was saying.

When John seemed to be done talking, Albert said. "Welcome to the club. I've been searching for answers and dreaming about today for longer than I can remember. I think it's what drove me to start writing. The only difference is I knew if I tried to tell the actual story, no one would believe me, so I kept it to children's stories."

And then he laughed. "So, John," he continued, "it's up to the five of us on this farm, along with a million seven-year-olds, to come up with an answer to the Orchard Walker mystery. In other words, why us, why now, and why Frank?"

Mom did not want to know the answer to her father's questions, so she announced that she was going to lie down with Adam.

As she got up, John crossed the porch and gave her a hug, then asked Albert if he wanted any more coffee. "I'm getting one for myself. I'm not ready to close my eyes yet. Actually, not sure if I will close my eyes tonight."

"No more for me, thank you," he said, glad that he was no longer getting yelled at. Then when the boy's parents went into the house, he turned to the woods and softly spoke to his grandson somewhere out in the night.

"Frank my boy, you have now become part of the cycle. Edalb will tell you it is the cycle of life, action, birth, and death.

Your father is not wrong. That you have been chosen for this journey to the middle meadow is no accident. Stay close to Edalb, Frank, and be careful. I am with you in spirit. I hope you can feel that."

SIXTEEN

Once they entered the woods, Frank and the clan gathered at an enormous tree. How big it actually was, Frank could not tell because everything was huge to him. He saw that the Orchard Walkers seemed to be relaxing and setting up a kind of camp.

"What's going on?" asked Frank. "Why have we stopped?"

Frank did not notice that Ria had come up with the last of the walkers, and she was the first to answer. "We will rest here until the sun comes up. We need to wait for the yawn.

"Yawn?" Frank asked.

Ria was getting comfortable with Frank and seemed surprised by the question. She held up both hands and said, "isn't this your farm?"

Frank was just as surprised by her reaction and said, "Well, yes. I mean it's my grandfather's farm. I've never heard him talk about the 'yawn'." Which Frank emphasized by using air quotes.

Ria looked around and realized that she was getting a lot of attention, so she relaxed a bit and said, "I get it. Okay, maybe that's not known to Notus. I thought any farmer would know about the yawn in the sunlight."

Confused, but relaxing a bit, Frank asked, "Yawn in the sunlight?"

Ria could see by the confused look on Frank's face that this was something new to the boy and so she spoke more slowly next.

She continued. "At night, all trees settle, and their energy is put into the roots. Once it gets dark, the roots expand with the stored energy that the tree has collected during the day."

Pointing upward, she continued. "During the day, this tree, and all the trees, will yawn, spreading their branches to gather as much energy from the sun as they can. During this yawn, the roots will shrink. When they shrink, I mean the roots, it creates a space between the root and the earth. These passages under the earth are what we use to travel about. And once we are past the entrance of the root tunnel, the spaces are wide open and stay that way. It's where the rainwater gathers and creates the springs."

Getting a little bit lost in her words, the green color of Ria's face lightened, and a huge smile appeared. I love it down there. So beautiful. We are more often under the orchard than above."

"So that's why we never see you!" Frank exclaimed. "There must be hundreds of places to hide during the day!"

"Not just to hide," Ria said. "When we travel along the roots, we have access to anywhere we want to go, except, that to the – "

"Yeah, I know…" Frank said, interrupting. "The Middle Meadow."

Edalb was enjoying the conversation between Ria and Frank and interrupted by saying, "But that will all change, soon." Startling Frank by seeming to come out of nowhere. "We have two days of travel before you head back home, and it will be your first time along the roots. Please rest. The day's yawn will come before you know it."

Edalb's advice was taken seriously, so Frank and the others all stopped talking, and Frank noticed a few walkers with swords seemed to be guarding the area, so Frank relaxed.

Before he fell asleep, he thought about the trees of his grandfather's orchard. Before now, no one had told him about how a tree can yawn, and was it his imagination, or was it easier to run between the trees after dark, after the yawn, and did he always get hit by branches when he ran through during the day?

'Weird,' thought Frank. *'And how do we travel along the roots of this tree? Where will it end? Is it safe?"* And then before his eyes closed, the last thing he thought was something he had never said during any other overnight camping trips. *'I think I would rather be home in bed.'*

SEVENTEEN

Back at the farm, as Frank's first day with the Orchard Walkers ended, Frank's Mother was sitting on the side of Adam's bed when he looked up and asked if Frank was home yet. "Not yet, tomorrow I hope, go back to sleep." She answered.

"I'm sorry about today," Adam told her.

"I know honey, don't worry, everything will be okay." And then she laid down next to Adam and fell asleep just as he did.

When Dad came out on the porch, he saw Grandpa looking over his old book. "Dad," he wondered, "do you think there are Orchard Walkers all over the place, or just here, in your orchard?"

Grandpa really didn't know. "Hard to tell really, according to what they told me, the original clan was broken up many years ago by what I think was an earthquake. Everything flooded and they ran for the hills. I guess it's these hills where they stayed since then. If there are more like them around the world, it never came up."

Pointing to the book, he continued. "I really don't know how they settled on the Middle Meadow, or how they found it, or any of the details. It's almost like their history doesn't jive with the history of the earth as we know it. We are taught that the core of the earth is warm, even hot. But I'm telling you, it's downright pleasant.

"Edalb talked about the history of the Orchard Walkers going back many, many years, but I was the first contact with humans that they had, it really made no sense to me then, and I haven't been able to put it together yet."

"Don't you know where this meadow is? Couldn't we dig to it?" Dad asked.

Albert got up to go into the house. "No, I don't. And I would be concerned about digging at random. That's why I want them gone. To get away from the gas company, and frankly all things that we consider modern. Lef them have their lives, and the peace all the creatures of the woods should have.

I spent a lifetime trying to reconnect, and seeking out these tunnel entrances, but everything looks different when you're so small. Your perspective is all," and then he waved his hands around. "It's all distorted. It's almost like when we look down to see them and can't, it's the same when they look up to see us and can't.

"It's been a long time since I had that view, so maybe I've forgotten a thing or two, but I will tell you one thing..." Grandpa said as both men went into the house. "Tomorrow I will look again; this time not for any orchard walker, but for my grandson."

He turned to his son-in-law and put his large, calloused hand on John's shoulder and said. "I know it won't come easy, but let's try to get some sleep, so we're fresh in the morning. Frank will be home tomorrow, so help me."

Dad took one last look at the woods. "I'm leaving the door open tonight. I don't think I'll be able to sleep anyway." And then after a brief pause, he said, "Dad, before you go up, there is one thing I wanted to ask you without Frank's mother overhearing..."

Grandpa was glad to hear his son-in-law call him, 'dad.' Maybe he wasn't angry with him anymore. "What's the question, John?"

"What about natural enemies in the woods for someone so small? Birds, weasels, snakes, animals like that?"

"That's interesting, John. This I do remember hearing Edalb speak about. How can I best put it. The Orchard Walkers are..." Grandpa searched for the right words. "The Orchard Walkers seem to be the purest part of nature; they are the innocents of the woods. They have spent hundreds of years living among and under all that we see when we look at a field of grass, a row of trees in an orchard, or even the darkest woods. All that time without making an enemy of any other beast."

Both men turned and looked into the darkness that surrounded the house as Albert continued. "As best as I can tell, they have no natural enemies. It's one reason, besides the fact that it's so hard to believe, that I never told anyone they were real before. I just knew that man and man alone could end up being the enemy of the Orchard Walker, not on purpose, but just by curiosity, needing to know more about them, perhaps hunting them just for the fun of it, and I never wanted to see that happen."

Grandpa squeezed John's upper arm then let it go and continued. "Have no fear for your son. I'm worried too, but less than you, because I believe in them and know they will watch out for our boy. Try to get some sleep John. See you bright and early, we'll find him."

As Dad sat down in the kitchen, looking out at the dark woods once again, a thought occurred to him. *'I've read every book that old man wrote. I never thought any of it could be real, and now this is too real, way too real. I hope this thing he calls Edalb is as good with his blade as the old man says he is.'*

EIGHTEEN

When Frank awoke the next day, it seemed that someone had put a leaf on him like a blanket. When he lifted the blanket off, he noticed that some dew drops had accumulated on the leaf. They looked like crystal softballs.

As he went to throw the leaf off, he heard someone say, “drink first! Drink from the morning mist. The morning dew will get you through.”

Thinking about it, and because he was thirsty, he figured he had nothing to lose so he sucked up one of the drops of water. Seeing how it was cool and refreshing, he tilted the leaf towards his face, and one by one the drops slapped him in the face. He didn’t catch all of it in his mouth, but he drank plenty, and it woke him up.

“I guess you’re ready?”

Frank turned and saw Quartz looking at him.

“Now or never!” Frank exclaimed.

“Yes. But never, never.” Quartz said.

Which made Frank realize once again how important today’s journey would be.

Last night, prior to going to sleep, the last thing Frank saw was the moon. Today when he looked up, the sky was blocked completely by the tree and its leaves.

Edalb had entered the small clearing and saw Frank looking up and around, and said, “You noticed, young Notus! The yawn has begun!”

It was true. Last night the tree limbs had huge gaps, but this morning, the branches were spread out almost entirely blocking the sun.

“I never noticed this before,” Frank said.

To which Edalb replied, “You’ve never been this small before. The closer we are to nature, the more we BE in nature, the more we SEE in nature.”

Then with a laugh that Frank had never heard from Edalb, the leader of the clan continued and said, “And how many times have you been in and among the roots of an apple tree?”

“Umm, never.”

“Exactly! Much more to learn and see. We will be leaving in a few moments. Let us know when you are ready.”

After a while, the clan gathered at the base of a nearby tree. As Frank watched, a bunch of Orchard Walkers moved close to where a big root entered the ground and pulled softly on the moss that covered the root. After a moment, they uncovered a hole in the ground large enough to walk through.

‘Well,’ Frank thought, *‘large enough for me to walk through now.’*

A few Orchard Walkers went in while everyone waited. Frank wondered if they were checking for animals or bugs or something. Returning after just a few moments, they signaled to the others who lined up ready to enter the hole in the moss.

Turning to Ria, Frank asked, “What’s that all about. Checking for danger?”

To which Ria responded, “Danger? No! Just checking that this root leads to a tunnel, a way in. You need to put your fear aside. The only thing to worry about is getting tired, or slipping in the mud,” and then after pointing to the pack on Frank’s back, she said, “or that the meadow twig knows what it’s doing?”

Frank was ignored when he asked, “What do you mean, that it knows what it’s doing?”

Not happy that no one cared about the question, and not wanting to be left alone, or to be the last one in line to enter the hole in the moss, Frank moved forward toward the huge tree.

One by one, each of the walkers got to the base of the root and disappeared into the hole as if just walking through the moss. When Frank got to the hole he stopped, afraid that the twisting hole seemed dangerous.

Turning to Edalb who was walking just behind him, Frank had questions. “What’s down there?” he said.

“The way home. Well… our home. But I know what you’re saying. Scary at first, but there is nothing to fear. You will be amazed by the fresh air, the wonderful water, and the bright lights. Yes, there are even lights. It is only dark here, where your world meets ours; I think nature’s way of keeping its secret.

"This is the opening to under the earth. It exists only during the yawn. It's a place very few have seen, the sub walker root tunnels, and when you return, and you will return home, to your home, you will have a story to tell your family. Like your grandfather did so many years ago."

Now remembering that his own grandfather was proof that this was something to trust and needing to trust this strange creature and wanting to help the walkers, Frank took a deep breath while looking up at the trees one last time and entered the moss cave.

When he took the first ten steps, he felt the rush of air coming from inside and heard the echo of the Orchard Walkers cheering, Notus, Notus, Notus.

Frank lost a little fear with each step he took. And then he saw the bright lights.

"What is this place?" Frank asked. "Where is all this light coming from?"

It was something Frank could not even imagine in one of his crazy dreams. Exiting the root tunnel and stepping out to a larger section of the root cave, Frank could see small streams of water that seemed to glow. Starting from a small pool, several streams of water seemed to go away from the center of the pool, with each stream following a root or coming from a root that Frank guessed fed the trees on the surface of the earth.

"Is each one of these roots from one of Grandpa's apple trees?" Frank asked. "And where is all this light coming from?"

Edalb seemed to be ready for the questions, and said, "I will do my best to show you things as we move forward, but the two questions you have now are some of my favorite things to talk about, because these are the secrets of the Orchard Walker's life."

"I won't tell anyone," Frank said.

"No matter!" Edalb replied, "you can share everything with anyone. The secrets of the underground are known by all the creatures who live, burrow, or hunt in these passages."

With a smile Edalb said, "It would not matter if people knew them as well."

Frank wondered if Grandpa knew, and never told.

Again, as if his mind were being read by Edalb, Edalb said, "even your grandfather would be surprised by what you learn while you are with us. He never had to take the journey a journey such as this. Yours is a mission."

Frank asked again about the light. "So… how is possible to be below ground, and for there to be so much light? It seems to come from nowhere, and everywhere, all at once."

"It does," said the elder Orchard Walker. And then he reached out and took Frank's hand and walked him over to the water's edge. "Dip your hand into the water. This water begins on the surface and follows the roots along their path. During the day, when the trees are in the yawn, and the roots shrink, it made not just the tunnels we travel, but also a place for the water to run. Since it is surface water and the sun is shining, the light reflects within the water itself and is carried along with the water to the earth below."

And then he emphasized it again. "Go ahead, dip your hands in, and drink some if you like."

Frank did as he was challenged. After dipping his hand in the water, Frank lifted some in his cupped hands and let it drop. When the water was in his hands, it was clear. The same color as when Frank would fill his hands with the garden hose. But when he dropped the water back into the small pond, it took on the light again and seemed to sparkle.

"It's okay to drink?" Frank asked.

"Yes, the earth has filtered it as pure as any water you have ever drank."

Frank took some again in his hands and slurped a mouthful. "Wow, it's so cold! I love it!"

As Frank helped himself to more handfuls of water, he pointed to the many roots that surrounded them.

"And these roots, they're from Grandpa's trees?"

Edalb and the others were happy to see Frank take the water, and they did the same. While Edalb was continuing to drink, Ria explained about the roots.

She began by jumping up on top of a brown root that came out of the earth like a big snake. "See this root?" she said, pointing to her feet. "See the bumps that run along the side here? This is one of your grandfather's trees. Which one, I do not know, but the bumps tell me it is a fruit tree."

She went on. "Other tree roots have scales, or are smooth, and some even appear to have legs, like centipedes." Then she did a little jump and slid down the side of the root, landing so close to Frank that he jumped back. "What's that word you use? Cool? Yeah, roots are cool!"

"And look!" Now she was on her knees pointing to the lower section of the root. "See this little guy? That's a root from a pine tree. Do you notice anything interesting?"

Frank knelt down, too, and looked closely at the two roots, and said, "they're connected?"

"They sure are," said Ria. "Once the roots get down here, they all join together, feeding off of each other, and supporting each other." Then she lightly punched Frank in the shoulder. "Wasn't I right? Cool roots, huh?"

Frank had to admit he had never given any of this any thought at all. It was kind of cool. Now refreshed and really wanting to get back to his family, and seeing how the dozens of roots that came together at this pond seemed like a maze, he asked Ria, "How do we know where to go? I really need to get home."

"That will be up to the stream," Edalb said while pointing to the pond, depending on the flow, maybe a full day, maybe less."

"The flow?" asked Frank. "What flow?"

"The flow of the spring, my friend. The flow of water will take the twig to the Deep Tree. The Meadow Twig will lead us."

"How can that be?" Frank asked. "What do you mean? The twig will lead us?"

Edalb came closer to Frank and as he put his hand on Frank's shoulder he removed the meadow twig from the small backpack. "Young Frank, as you can see, we are at a hub." And Frank's gaze followed Edalb's as they looked around.

In front of them was the small pond surrounded by several roots that seemed to be drinking from the pond. From there the roots got larger and larger and headed off into the tunnels that took them back to the base of the tree.

Edalb explained. “Some of these tunnels will take us to the surface of the orchard, and some will take us deep into the earth, but one of them will take us to the roots of the Deep Tree, which will lead us to the Middle Meadow and the end of the journey.”

“So which way do we go?” To Frank, they all looked the same.

“We can search each of them. We can send an Orchard Walker to examine each root and its tunnel and hope that someone stumbles upon it and knows what to look for.”

Looking around at the dozens of roots that Frank guessed were drinking from the pond, he became worried that Edalb’s plan seemed like it would take forever.

As Frank was about to express his doubt, Edalb raised his hands that held the strange, round, twig that Frank had been carrying. He rotated the ring of wood as he said, “Or, as I have said, we can let the twig show us the way.”

Edalb could tell by Frank’s expression that the boy was confused. “Frank,” he said, “this twig you brought back to us is a growing thing. Its parent tree is still a growing thing, as well.”

Edalb continued, “In order to populate a forest, a tree gives back to nature five things. A sucker sprout, a water sprout, a seed, and if you can find one, a flyer.

A sucker sprout grows out of the base of the tree. Just under where the bark touches the ground. You can see them all over your grandfather's orchard. They are young trees trying to mimic the mother plant.

A water sprout grows just above the sucker sprout, it's not a limb, but more like a root that is seeking a place to grow. Sometimes they will bow down and meet the earth to plant themselves.

Then come the seeds, as you know. They come from a flower, a cone, or the fruit that grows on the mother tree. Like the apples we will soon enjoy at the Deep Tree your family calls Old Rusty"

Frank held up the twig that Edalb had handed him. "And what is this twig?" He asked.

Edalb pointed at the Meadow Twig. "That you have in your hand Notus is a rarity among plant growth. Have you taken a good look at it? You hold what is known as a flyer, the circular stem of a growth knot. It both contributes food to itself and feeds off itself." Edalb smiled. "Look more closely, it also has a remarkable, magical ability."

Frank stared down at the twig and saw that the bark around the twig was moving ever so slightly as if growing around and around into itself. Frank scratched a loose flake of the bark off into his hand. The gap in the bark healed itself almost immediately. The small piece that landed in his hand turned to dust and blew away.

"Magic?" he asked.

"Yes. For you see young one, the flyer twig from the growth knot of the Deep Tree has an amazing ability."

And with that Edalb reached out and took the twig from Frank and tossed it in the pond.

It sailed through the air spinning like a coin tossed into a wishing well. When it struck the water, as Frank gasped, it went straight to the bottom. The circular splash became a round ripple that came to the shore and disappeared.

Frank couldn't believe what he saw. "We came all this way to throw it away! Why am I even here?"

"It sunk!" Frank screamed. "What do we do now?"

Edalb almost ignored Frank, and just kept looking at the middle of the pond, and said, "Notus, after one hundred and twenty of our years, we have the time to give it a moment, wait and see."

Frank worried and stared at the water, eventually, the twig came to the surface. Frank stared back at Edalb in amazement.

"Not to worry!" Edalb exclaimed. "Not to worry! The magic of the twig, as every Orchard Walker knows, is the amazing ability to find its parent tree."

Edalb looked back again at the water. "It's on the move! We're off!" Sure enough, the little round twig began to float into one of the many tunnels.

Frank could not believe what he saw and could barely keep up with Edalb as he hopped and ran down the bank of the small river. As Frank watched the twig in the water, something did not seem right. "Edalb!" he shouted, "the twig is going against the current! That's just not possible!"

Edalb stopped long enough to turn and reply. "This is not your world, young Frank. The Notus knows not all. Welcome to the world of the Orchard Walker. Welcome to my world. Our world." Then he turned, "come now! We're very close!"

But not as close as they thought. Obviously unable to climb out and cross over to the next stream, when the twig came to an obstacle Edalb leaned in and then threw it into the next body of water, and the chase began again.

Frank could not tell how long it had been since the race along the bank had begun. The Orchard Walkers did their best to clear a path in the tunnel along the stream taking care not to get too close, fearful that they would fall in the water.

"Beware of your step, Notus," Edalb said. "And keep careful look out for the Enots."

While looking over his shoulder, Frank told Edalb what he had been thinking. "They must be miles from here; we haven't seen them since early last night."

"So true," said the Carrier of the Blade, "But remember, now we are making a path for them to follow. They are sure to run across it and begin to follow, perhaps staying at a distance until we get to the Deep Tree."

"I hadn't thought of that," Frank said, checking once more over his shoulder. Seeing nothing, he relaxed a bit and continued on.

"And be careful of the ring of grass around your neck. If it should catch on a small root and be pulled off of you or broken, we will lose you, and never make it home."

Fingering the blades of grass that made up the ring around his neck, Frank remarked, “I hadn’t thought of that either. What would happen if I got big underground?”

“We aren’t that far underground yet,” said Edalb. “You would probably pop up in a field and scare your parents!”

Edalb could not know how much Frank was missing his parents. *‘I don’t know if that would be so bad’* Frank said to himself.

In the meantime, the twig kept moving.

As Frank and the clan made their way along the bank of the river, the twig made its way between the rocks as it coursed upstream toward the Deep Tree somewhere in the distance.

All eyes were forward; Edalb kept his on the twig, Frank kept his eyes on Edalb, and while the clan of Orchard Walkers made their way along the tunnels created by the roots, they could not know that the Enots were looking forward as well; to a meeting with the clan that had taken too many years to finally happen.

As Edalb had predicted, the Enots did find a strange little footprint and realized it was from the Notus that was with them. The Enots did not have a magic twig to guide them through the underground, and as it turned out, fate or luck had been with them. Just up ahead was the entire Orchard Walker clan, minus the Enots of course, and among them would be the boy, the boy that brought back the missing twig that would see them home to the Middle Meadow, all of them.

Every time they found another of Frank’s footprints, it energized the Enots, and they marched forward as if on a mission.

NINETEEN

Mom did not sleep well at all the night before and really wasn't surprised to see the three men of the house come down shortly after she made some coffee and put some bread in the toaster. "Adam, you're up awfully early, can I get you some cereal?"

"Yeah, thanks, I wonder what Frank is eating for breakfast."

"Food coals, I suspect," his grandfather said. "You should know that... you read the books."

Adam's mother made a 'yuck' expression as Adam asked, "What do they taste like Grandpa?" Adam asked, "I bet Frank won't eat em."

Not able to control herself any longer, Lynn said, "This is all so hard to believe, I'm worried sick. I still can't get over the fact that Frank spent the night in the woods with these things that I always thought were just make believe. Remind me what these food thingies are made from anyway?"

"Well," Grandpa started to answer, "Some Orchard Walkers are in charge of collecting the twigs for the food coal fires. Each coal fire has some special twigs that don't turn to ash, but instead turn into food coals while the fire is burning."

"That's one reason the Middle Meadow was so special; aside from the meadow being away from the surface for protection, the springs that bring water to the meadow also bring a ton of these special twigs. But to answer your question, when the fire is out, these coals that are left over are what they eat."

"Yuck!" said Adam. "So, like the end of my stick when I roast a marshmallow?"

Grandpa was surprised by the accuracy of Adam's description and said, "Actually, that's pretty close."

"How terrible!" said Mom.

"What do they taste like?" asked Dad.

"Believe it or not, not bad," said Grandpa. "If I remember correctly, kind of feels like an apple in your mouth that tastes like soda pop."

"Cool!" said Adam. "Wish I could have some!"

Dad winked at Adam. "We could make a mint selling those, hey?"

Mom wasn't listening anymore and pointed a big fork at Dad and said, "When you're done hoping I serve sticks for lunch when are you guys going out to look for our son?" Mom was growing more worried thinking now that Frank hadn't eaten anything but sticks for two days. "What is your plan?"

Dad stood up and drank the last of his juice. "Albert and I are going to the river. He'll go down stream, and I'll work my way up. Somewhere there has to be an entrance to the river that surrounds this 'middle meadow' place. I don't see how we'll miss them. If they are still on the surface, we'll find him, I promise." Then he kissed his wife on the cheek and headed for the front door.

"Come on Dad!" he called.

But before he could get out, Mom stopped him and asked, "And what if they are not on the surface. What if they are underground?"

Realizing what she had just thought, she turned to her father. "Dad, is that even possible? That he is somewhere under the orchard?"

Picking up his hat and placing it on his head, Grandpa saw the worry in his daughter's eyes. He did not want to make her any more worried, and just said, "One thing at a time." But he knew the honest answer.

Adam jumped up from his chair. "I'm going with you! Wait for me!"

Dad thought that maybe Adam would want to come, but also thought it best that not too many people came out today, not wanting to scare the Orchard Walkers away or make the Enots mad.

"No son," he said to Adam. "You stay here and take watch of the house. We need someone to come and get us if Frank gets home before we do."

"Rats! Stay at home. Stay at home, that's me, Mr. Stay at home. I don't get to eat food coals or nothin!"

Grandpa felt bad for Adam. Even though he was old, he wished that he could be out with Frank, too. "Listen, we don't need your help as much as your mother does, stay here with her."

"If you like, you can help by going up to my writing room and use the sight glass to keep a watch on the lawn and the woods. From my corner room, you'll be able to track both of us all the way up to Old Rusty. From that window, you'll be able to see more than we will."

"Really? Cool!" Adam exclaimed. Grandpa never let anyone touch the stuff in his writing room. It was the coolest room Adam had ever seen, and he ran right up the stairs to start the search.

Lynn said to her father, "Be careful Dad." Then she turned to her husband. "John?"

"I know, I know, don't worry. I feel really good about it. He'll be back today."

Grandpa interrupted. "I can feel it… today's the day."

Dad reached out and held his wife's hand. "I know you'll call us if you hear or see anything. We'll see you later."

So, the men headed off for the woods, and the river beyond. Dad was hoping that he was right and that he would see his son very soon.

Grandpa was more certain. "It feels right," he thought. "Either I'm becoming one of them, or I've been taken over by the cycle, as well, but it feels right. Today's the day for sure."

As Grandpa moved a branch out of his way, he looked at the small leaves poking through the outer bark and muttered, "My trees are growing really well, and I'm hot on the trail of the Orchard Walker clan. I feel like a young man again. Just let those Enots try to get in my way."

TWENTY

Impossible to know what time it was, Frank was getting worried about maybe having to spend another night out without his family. He and the Orchard Walkers had just come out from a tunnel facing another maze of roots leading away from the small body of water. The twig seemed to stall in the center of the pond.

It gave Frank a chance. “Edalb, I have to rest. My feet are killing me!” Frank said as he slid down the smooth surface of one of the roots and leaned against it.

“If we rest,” said Edalb, “We will lose sight of the Meadow Twig, and maybe the Enots will catch up to us. I’ve been impressed with the progress we’ve made along the root tunnels, but we are not alone down here; do you think they haven’t noticed?”

Ignoring him, Frank said, “Maybe this will help,” and he slid down the bank a bit and stuck both of his feet into the river and let them dangle in the chilly water.

“Ahhh, just for a minute, Edalb. This feels great.” Frank closed his eyes and swirled his feet in the water.

“Frank… Frank.” Edalb was trying to get Frank’s attention.

“Just a minute… I promise.”

“Look at your foot, Frank!” Edalb exclaimed. “No need to wait a minute anymore!”

Frank opened his eyes and looked down at his feet in the water. Floating near his right foot was the Meadow Twig. It had come ashore when Frank closed his eyes. "OH MY GOSH! Edalb! Should I throw it back in?"

Edalb smiled for the second time that day. "We are here, Notus. Take the twig out of the water. We have arrived at the Deep Tree. That is the root that must lead to the core. It is time."

As Edalb secured the twig once again in Frank's pack Frank asked, "Do you really think so?" And then pointed down the nearby tunnel. "So, we follow this root…"

"Yes! Quick now. Before we are seen by the enemy."

Now with much more energy than he had before, Frank, as well as all of the Orchard Walkers almost ran into the large tunnel by the Deep Tree root.

Before leaving the small clearing, Edalb called for Quartz and said, "You know what to do. We never stopped here."

And Quartz did know what to do. Using his hands, Quartz cupped water from the pond and began to sprinkle it on the path, erasing their footprints. As the last one to leave the clearing, he pushed the dirt, and sprinkled water so that there was no trace. Satisfied that the Enots would not know which root was the path, Quartz rushed to join the others, who were making their way to the core.

As the clan reached the core, or central root of the Deep Tree, Frank noticed that the core root seemed to have steps carved into it. Having been abandoned and not used in over 60 years, the steps were splintered and difficult to climb, so they all took care as they made their way up.

"I thought the Meadow was down," Frank said. "Why are we going up?"

Ria spoke up since Edalb was too far down the steps to hear. "We need to check the yawn. If it's too late in the day and go under, the roots will fill in the tunnel and you may not get out today. If we see that the sun still has time, and that the yawn will continue, we will have plenty of time to get to the meadow, find our way home, and get you back to your family." Moving now with skill and determination further up the steps, she added excitedly, "It won't be long now."

Frank was worried about the answer to the next question but asked it anyway. "What if it's too late in the day?"

Ria had heard the stress in Frank's voice but needed to be honest with her new friend, so she stopped climbing, and looked directly at Frank as she said, "We will have to wait until tomorrow."

"That's what I was afraid of," he said, with his head hanging low.

"Let's move!" It was Edalb calling from behind. "I need to see the sun!"

Moments later, one by one, the Orchard Walkers came into the sunlight. The core root had lead them to the top of the Deep Tree. When Frank came out from a hole in the bark of Old Rusty, he found himself standing in a cloud of leaves overlooking the farm, the farmhouse, and even the Hudson River off in the distance.

"Oh man, my grandpa is going to be mad."

"About what?" asked Ria. She knew there could be several answers.

"I'm not allowed to climb this tree!"

Ria looked around and laughed, but could think of nothing to say except, "Well, you are here now. I think it will be okay."

Then Frank heard, "Perfect!" It was Edalb followed by Quartz exiting the small hole in Old Rusty.

Then Edalb took a seat on the leaves. The trees canopy of leaves was so thick each branch seemed to be holding huge pillows of ancient apple leaves. Hanging below each of the pillows were huge rust-colored apples.

Those that had swords took them out from around their waists and cut apples from above. Edalb did the same, but almost without looking tossed his sword above Frank causing an apple to almost fall in the space between he, Ria, and Quartz. It was as if a giant beachball had dropped next to him. The apple was soft, and Frank was able to pry pieces off to eat.

"So sweet!" he exclaimed as he dug in.

"It's been too long," said the leader of the clan.

"Edalb," Frank asked with his head almost inside an apple, "when you said it was perfect, what did you mean?"

Edalb got up and took a seat next to Frank. "Perfect timing. To rest, to eat, and yes, my friend. Plenty of time to get to the Middle Meadow before dark."

Frank leaned back with a huge chunk of apple in his hand. "Then I agree. It's perfect!"

TWENTY-ONE

While Frank lay there, an Orchard Walker he did not know came over and gave him what looked like a root. "Chew on this." He said. Frank smelled the stick. It had a familiar smell, so he licked it. "Wow, licorice… thanks!"

As Frank chewed the root, it reminded Frank of trips to the store for candy, and how much he missed his brother and sister. He guessed it would not be long before they got to the meadow and said goodbye. He thought it was time to ask the questions that have been bugging him.

"Edalb," he began. "Tell me more about the cycle. I want to know more about your world, and I don't know anything."

Edalb, it seemed, had been waiting for the question, and began with a smile.

"The easiest way to explain the cycle," Edalb began, "is to think of it as kind of like your memory, but in reverse. It is the way things will happen to all living things but hasn't happened yet. All things affect everything else, and then come around again in a cycle. You see them when you see them, but you look carefully, can see them even before that."

"Each cycle is only a small part of the larger cycle of the universe. Examples surround us each day. You saw for yourself how the rain falls, gathers in the grass, and what the grasses do not need, causes the rain to enter the root tunnels."

"At the base of each living plant, there is a pool, sometimes large, sometimes small. All roots eventually join, or at least share the many pools of rainwater, which then enters the root, runs like a river inside the tree, then drips on the leaf you slept under last night, evaporates into the sky, becomes a cloud, and falls as rain."

Using both hands to point towards the horizon, he exclaimed, "Imagine the complexity of the cycles that surround us each day! Just as the cycle of the Orchard Walker in the grass put you here with us, the cycle of a small moth affects the cycle of the moon, itself."

This was sounding too much like science and Frank really didn't understand, but asked, "How can a moth affect the moon?"

Edalb leaned in toward Frank and looked him directly in the eyes and sounded again like his brother Adam's troll voice when he whispered. "Notus... how can it not!"

Frank thought it might be best to change the subject. "Uh, tell me about the blade around your waist."

Edalb wanted Frank to think about the lesson in the cycle, so he didn't answer the young Notus. Instead, Edalb leaned back and looked at the sky. There was still plenty of time to talk and travel later.

After taking more apple, and handing a piece to Ria and Quartz, Frank said, "Tell me about your blade, Edalb, is it magic?"

"Magic?" said Edalb, "I wouldn't call it magic. I was chosen to be the carrier of the blade, so I carry it, and since I carry it, I am Edalb. It has been this way since the big shake and flood."

"I did not know the power of the blade until the shake began. A large tree was about to fall on me, and I don't know why I did it, but I held the blade over my head and yelled, BLADE, CUT FOR ME. The tree, when it hit the blade, fell into two pieces at my feet. I would have been killed. That's the secret of the blade."

"Wait, what is the secret? Can you tell me?" Frank hoped.

Edalb studied the young Notus in front of him and thought a change was taking place. What he once might have thought to be silly questions, somehow seemed to become important. Something was moving Edalb to share.

"I have found in my many years," began the carrier of the blade, "that you can carry the blade and be the Edalb, but the power of the blade is not yours until you use the blade to save your own life, or the life of someone you love."

"So, the first one who had the blade, his name was Edalb, too?" Frank reached around to his back and wished he had a blade, instead of the ring in his pack.

"It's not like that," Edalb said to Frank. "I am called Edalb, but it is as much my name as it is my title. It is what I am. I am the keeper of the blade. Blade spelled backward is Edalb. I am not Edalb as much as I am the blade itself. We are one. Without it, I am no longer Edalb."

"Many of the words the Orchard Walkers began to use after taking your language are said backwards. I do not know the origin of this."

Frank thought about this and the Orchard Walkers he knew. "Oh, like Ria, is air. K-cor, the little guy who loved Adam's shirt, is rock. Ert?"

Then they all heard a voice call out, “It has two ‘e’s’.”

To which Fank responded, “Oh... Ert is tree. Rewolf, then is flower. Mica… hey what about Mica and Quartz?”

“I didn’t say all The Orchard Walkers. They took the names of Earth's basic beauty and strength.”

“What about the Enots, do they have names?”

“I’m sure they do, but I don’t recall. We call them Enots, backwards for stone. It reminds us of how they stole our food and replaced our food with stones. Back after the big shake as we protected ourselves in the hills, they took our food, then left us during the night.”

“It was on the third night. I don’t know what came over them. While we slept on the mountain, they came as silent as owls and took our food. We have been enemies since. These Enots, who left us on the mountain to starve.”

Edalb took a moment and looked around. “We would eventually make our way to the Middle Meadow. Just ready to head out. They put stones in our sacks of food coals.” Then he whispered, remembering the day like it was yesterday, “We barely made it to the Deep Tree core, where we had to wait for the waters to go down before we could find the tunnels to the meadow.”

Frank thought for a moment. “Weren’t there any trees up on the mountain to make food coals?”

“Fruit trees, Frank. Fruit trees!” Edalb raised his voice. “Must be the bark of two-year growth in order to have the coals just right.”

"Two-year growth?" Frank asked. "What's two-year growth?"

Edalb stopped and looked back, and said, "has the great notus taught you nothing?"

Then after grabbing a branch of a tree, he brought it to Frank's face. "What do you see, Notus?"

"A branch?"

"Look closer, see the green?"

"I see a tiny branch growing out of a bigger branch." Frank was nodding his head.

Edalb's eyes lit up. "Yes, yes, see the small green growth of this year? The branch it comes from is last year. Last year's limb is called second-year growth. Now go back to where it connects to the larger limb, that's now three years old, and so on, and so on."

Frank got up, reached out and broke the small branch off of the tree and held it up. "So, I can make food coals out of this?"

"Yes! If only you knew how." Then Edalb pointed to the branches that surrounded them all and said, "So protect them Frank, protect them for us, and for your grandfather as well. The second-year twigs, Notus! They feed me, they feed Quartz, Ria, the rest, and they feed your grandfather!"

"What are you saying, Edalb." Grandpa isn't an Orchard Walker."

With that Edalb laughed and pointed to the apples that were hanging above Frank's head. "Isn't he, Frank? Isn't he?"

Confused, Frank looked in the direction where Edalb had pointed. A dozen apples hung in a row, and above them, many more. As Frank looked around, he gasped.

All the apples were hanging from second year growth.

"Wait, Edalb, are all these apples growing on second year twigs?"

"They do. So is your grandfather an Orchard Walker, a creature of nature whose food comes from second year growth, or is he not?"

"That kind of freaks me out. I never thought about it like that. I wonder if Grandpa does. Edalb, do you think my grandfather knows how closely related he is to you, I mean to the clan?

"Of course he does young notus. He knows very well. Why else would he have sent you here?

"What are you talking about? It was a dream that started this. I told you."

"Ah, but a dream you dreamed while asleep in your grandfather's house, while he, too, was asleep. Think about it. Think about the wings of our friend the moth. Think about the drop of dew you drank this morning that had come from the tunnels you walked later today."

"Things have a way of impacting things. Did you dream your dream, or was it his dream?"

Still not sure of what Edalb was talking about, Frank decided to change the subject and said, “Wait, I have another question. It’s about something you said down in the tunnels.”

Edalb seemed to be in a talkative mood, and liked that Frank was showing interest in the world around him, so he was happy to reply by saying, “What do you recall me saying in the tunnels?”

Counting on his hand, Frank said, “You said that a tree gave back five things. But then you only mentioned four. You said sucker sprout, water sprout, seeds, and a flyer. That’s only four.”

Edalb turned away from Frank and looked again out at the orchard below.

“I was waiting for this and hoped you would bring your question at this time, to this very place.”

Frank followed Edalb’s gaze and faced the many trees, and hills in the distance. Something inside himself knew that Edalb was not done with his explanation, so he said nothing, and just waited.

Frank saw that others in the clan had gathered and were silently listening.

“The fifth thing, is the most critical.” Edalb began. “The fifth thing that a tree gives is the final thing that a tree gives. It gives itself.”

Frank was about to ask something when Edalb raised his hand and continued. “Frank. When a tree is done. When a tree has given all it can give. It gives the only thing left to give. It no longer produces any of the other four. No longer able to push a sucker sprout, a water sprout, a seed, or ever a flyer, and then one cool year, it drops each leaf, leaves that will never return. Then in the warm year, one by one, it gives a limb, which drops to the earth, becomes dust, and part of the earth."

"Then the tree itself will fall, becoming one with the soil as it too becomes a dust that scatters on the field becoming the bed for the next generation of trees."

"It is the cycle I spoke of. Something I am afraid many have lost the ability to read or see."

In the quiet of the moment, Edalb turned to his young friend and pointed at Frank. He said, "But not you. You are here for a reason. Perhaps you are here to learn more than just how to get home. Maybe you are here to learn how to keep a home. How to grow one with the earth."

And after a pause, Edalb whispered. "Perhaps you are here to become an Orchard Walker. A guardian to the Deep Tree… the one you call," as he tapped the tree limb on which they were sitting. "Old Rusty!"

Edalb had given Frank a lot to think about and even though he had many more questions, Frank kept quiet as he rested and looked out over the farm. In a way, he realized, his granddad was an Orchard Walker. He spent his life walking the orchard, making a living off the apples that grew on the same twigs that created food coals. Frank began to realize how important his grandfather's work was.

Looking out from his high place in the Deep Tree, the trees that Frank had seen during each visit had changed. Frank still saw them as the place where Paige, Adam and he used to play, but from the top of Old Rusty, Frank began to see it as a different place.

He saw squirrels rushing around gathering leaves. He saw deer standing on their hind legs eating the berries that surrounded the orchard, and he saw birds taking flight from the tops of the trees to begin their migration south for the winter.

Something stirred in Frank. He no longer saw a farm, but a living breathing thing. *'It's like another planet down there.'* He thought to himself. *'Is this why I'm here?'*

"Edalb!" Frank exclaimed, maybe a little too loudly. "I have to save this place. For Grandpa… and for you!"

"Save it from who?" Ria asked. Coming up to his side.

"The oil men!" Frank exclaimed. They want to destroy the farm for the oil and gas underneath. "The state says they will take the farm from Grandpa if -"

Interrupting Frank, Edalb gave him a wink, and said, "Notus, I've been underneath." And then he paused and held out his hands, which were empty. As Frank stared at the mitt-like hands, Edalb said, "There's nothing there."

Frank looked up. "No oil?"

Ria responded. "I… think that's what he said."

"No gas?" Now Frank was getting really hyper now.

"You spent the day underground." Edalb told him. "Have you ever breathed in a cleaner air?"

"That's my name!" said Ria, and it made everyone laugh.

It was the best news Frank had heard in his life. Excitedly, he said, "I have to tell my family!"

"Edalb," Frank began, and then thought, *'Wait, am I actually saying this out loud?'*

Then Frank told all the Orchard Walkers, "I think… no, I know it. I want to be a farmer." Hardly believing his own voice, Frank gulped and said, "I want to spend my life walking this orchard."

Edalb walked slowly away and turned before entering the hole in the mighty tree's trunk. "Then," he said quietly, "let's get moving."

TWENTY-TWO

Up in Grandpa's writing room Adam had set himself up in the curved corner where the two walls formed half of a circle. Looking out the window on the left, he had a full view of the driveway, the lawn, and in the distance, the brook by the barn.

As the brook moved across the field, it grew larger as the little springs added water, and eventually disappeared into the woods. Adam used his grandfather's scope to get really close to the spring that came out from under Old Rusty.

"It's amazing how the water just keeps coming out of the ground." Adam said, but no one was there to hear him.

He ducked behind the curtains when he saw the men down in the stream using a small crane on the back of a truck to pull the wire spool out of the brook. Clean white boards had been nailed over the hole in the wall that was made yesterday during the sleigh ride down the hill.

To Adam, it seemed like a week had gone by, but it was only yesterday. The men did not look so happy. Adam decided to stay out of sight for a while.

The scope that Grandpa had was special and he never let Adam, or his brother use it unless he was with them. Adam remembered how Grandpa would let them into the room late at night and use it to look at the stars and the moon.

Adam never thought that it could be used during the day, but now he noticed that when he aimed the telescope at the lawn, and turned the black ring to focus, it made everything so big he could fill the entire view with just a few pieces of grass.

'He's been using this thing to watch the Orchard Walkers,' thought Adam. When he swung the scope into the orchard, he was able to catch his father and grandfather just as they went from the field into the orchard.

Down on the ground, as the two searchers began to spread out Grandpa had a thought and said, "Be sure to stay on this side of the river. They won't cross it because they can't swim."

"I remember," Dad replied. "I've been thinking though. I think we should walk in the water by the edge. That way, we won't step on them by accident. Does that make any sense to you?"

"Very good idea, John," Grandpa agreed. "Why not let's walk for an hour, and then meet back at the house to see if there's any news."

"I'll go up stream, you go down," Franks Father said. But as he stepped in the water, both men looked down when they heard "SNAP!"

"What was that?" Grandpa asked.

John looked down under his foot. "It was just a stick. Well, I'll see you in a little while."

"Okay, see you in a bit." Then Grandpa remembered something else. "And John, don't bother calling out Frank's name. You would never be able to hear him answer, and if they hear you coming, they will hide, sure as shoot!"

"Glad you told me, I never thought of that!"

So. the two men began the search on what was now the second day. Frank's Father was a little less worried, now that he thought he was close to finding him, but still, he had plenty on his mind and hoped that Frank would be home soon.

Albert also wanted to bring Frank home safe and sound. He also hoped the Orchard Walkers would be home when they found him. He hated the fact that this would be the Orchard Walkers' last chance.

'Being on the meadow is their only shot of surviving these darn fracking drills,' he thought.

Looking down toward the bank of the river and slowly moving along the edge, he muttered to himself, "I wish I had never even heard of an Orchard Walker."

TWENTY-THREE

After hearing it was time to go, Frank took one last look around as he stood on the highest spot in the orchard. The wind was calm below, but further up in the canopy of the huge tree, the branches were swaying. The leaves were almost musical to Frank as he listened to the wind and saw the huge apples move among the branches.

A moment ago, he had heard himself say that he was going to follow his grandfather and become a farmer. If it were true that the gas company would soon give back the orchard, he knew his grandfather would need help, and he had a lot to learn.

In the meantime, the Enots were stuck. After arriving at the last pond and looking around, they could not tell where to go next. They searched around the pond and saw that the footprints had been erased. Afraid they had lost the trail of the young Notus, one of the Enots saw a strange mark on a root and looked down.

The mark that the Enot was looking at was made when Frank leaned up against the root, slid down, and dunked his feet into the pond. After looking more closely, they took a chance and chose that root to follow through the earth.

Fairly quickly, they came upon the staircase and instead of going up, like the Orchard Walkers had, the Enots went down. Down to find the Orchard Walkers before they took the Middle Meadow, or to find a place to hide and wait, while the Orchard Walkers rested among the branches above.

Two hours after the Enots had found the stairs and begun their journey to the bottom of the Deep Tree, Frank turned to look at the giant apple core that he left behind, took one last glance at the tree, the farm, and the Orchard Walkers that surrounded him. Then Frank followed Edalb into the hole in the tree without hesitation this time.

A lot had changed in a single day, and he felt stronger and perhaps for the first time he knew his mission.

'I'm going to get them to the meadow, and then I'm going home.' Frank said to himself.

Down they went, with Ria leading the way. The stairwell that seemed to be carved into the core of the tree went down and down. Frank had read about the stairs in the Statue of Liberty and wondered if they were similar.

'It's really tight in here. When does this end?' he thought.

Every ten steps or so, the turns that created the stairwell became so tight Frank had to twist his body to pass through. Always aware of the ring of weeds around his neck, he was careful not to get it caught. He shuddered wondering what would happen if he went back to his regular size if he was still in the middle of the tree. He didn't want to think about it, but thinking about it kept him careful.

After a while, the stairs got wider, and soon enough, the staircase got wider and opened into a huge room with another pond.

"Another pond?" Frank said aloud. "Edalb, when will we ever get there?"

Edalb turned and pointed to a root, and said, "Does this look familiar?"

At first Frank didn't see it, but as he got closer to the bump in the side of the root, he saw what looked like a knot in a tree.

"This round hole…" and then he reached behind to his pack and pulled out the Meadow Twig. Holding it up to the round bump in the root, he turned to the Orchard Walkers and said, "I think this would fit!"

"I know it will fit," Edalb replied, "I saw how well it fit when your grandfather took it out!"

It was true. The hole in the tree was the same shape and size as the donut shaped twig he held in his hand.

"It must go in here." Frank said. "Do I just, like… put it in? Is there a trick to it?"

By now, many, many The Orchard Walkers had gathered around the central root of the Deep Tree. What was once a fairly large space got smaller and smaller as more and more Orchard Walkers exited from the stairs and into the clearing.

'I don't remember seeing this many,' Frank thought. More than Frank had even seen before. Many more than he thought walked with him on the journey.

Edalb didn't seem to notice and spoke to the crowd. He started by speaking directly to Frank.

"Notus, this is truly a great day. As the Meadow Twig was removed by your grandfather, the order of the twig and of the Deep Tree is as true now as it was then."

“Once removed from the Deep Tree by someone who was not an Orchard Walker, only someone who is not an Orchard Walker may put it back, and for that time to come, the time being now, we have waited long and will wait no longer.”

“Frank, as I am the leader of the Orchard Walker clan, I ask you to do this for us, so we may return to our home on the Middle Meadow.”

Frank turned around slowly, and it hit him how important this was for his new friends. All this had started when his grandfather was a boy like him. Way before he was even born. They looked back at him with wonder in their eyes.

“Young Notus, we owe you so much. It took great courage to bring us the key to our home, and for that we are forever grateful.” And then Edalb motioned with his hands toward the ring of bark in front of Frank. “Let’s go. There is no time like now, and it is time.”

Frank bent down to see exactly how the ring of wood would fit into the hole in the tree. As he moved it closer to the knot hole, the bark on the ring began to move more quickly and the ring on the root seemed to shrink. When he had it matched up correctly, he started to put the twig into place when…

Suddenly an Orchard Walker was yelling, “NOOOO!” and grabbed the twig out of Frank’s hands. Frank was so startled he fell backwards.

“Enots!” Edalb yelled. “Drop the Meadow Twig, Enot, you have no claim!”

‘Enots?’ Frank thought. *‘It looks just like an orchard Walker, not horrible at all! What’s going on?’* Frank was lifting

himself up and just about to turn to Edalb and ask him how he knew it was an Enot when Edalb's blade flew right by Frank's head.

"Blade! Knock him!" Edalb yelled, and the blade flew toward the Enot holding the twig. As it approached, the blade turned sideways and instead of cutting, the blade knocked him and the twig into the water.

Almost as if the Enot were a stone himself, he sank as quickly as the Meadow Twig, completely out of sight. Frank could hear the crowd raising their voices. Blades were out pointing at each other.

To Frank it was a confusing sight, Orchard Walker against Orchard Walker. He looked at the water, the twig had surfaced, but the thief had not.

Frank could only think of one thing to do, and so he dove into the river to save both the Enot and the twig. After grabbing the twig, Frank was able to find the Enot under the water, and using the twig as a life saver, Frank swam him to the shore. Both of whom had gone in the water stood in the shallow water by the edge.

Edalb's sword had once again returned, and he held it out prepared to battle pointing at both Frank and whoever it was that he dragged from the river.

Both Enots and The Orchard Walkers pushed forward to see the daring rescue. The water was calm and not so deep but seeing the boy swimming was such an unusual sight even the most powerful of the Orchard Walkers lowered their swords as mouths opened in surprise. Every one of them seemed to be in a trance.

All of them were struck by Frank's courage and skill. Edalb remained alert watching over his clan. Frank helped the stranger out of the water after tossing the twig on the ground. As the Enot crawled up the bank of the river, he managed to capture the twig once more in his arms.

Alarmed and surprised after the rescue, the Orchard Walkers did not like that the Enot still held onto the Meadow Twig. Edalb raised his sword.

Out of the corner of his eyes, Frank could see Quartz's blade rise as well. "Stop!" he said. "Don't you see? They're just like you! I can't tell them apart from an Orchard Walker. Are they Enots, or Orchard Walkers? You have been separated for so long you forgot that they were once a part of the clan!"

Edalb interrupted Frank. "No young Notus. Here you are wrong. You cannot see what we see. Have you forgotten about the days on the mountain? We were left to starve."

"They went back for you, Edalb," the twig holder interrupted. "I was told that the food coals were taken to feed the rescue party that went back to save the Edalb. This was before my day and only a few remain of us that were there."

Edalb kept his guard up but took a step closer. "What do you mean they went back for me? I was at the top of the mountain. This is nonsense."

"Listen, please. Here is what I know," he continued, "we had barely escaped from the lower lands and had lost our swords and food. Everything was lost. When my group got to the mountain, we were told that the Edalb had not escaped, that you were missing."

"My clan decided at once to return to the valley, but we were starving, and without swords to cut wood or fuel for any fires. The water was rising, and we thought you were in trouble."

"According to what I was told, a decision was made. They took the food from your group knowing more could be produced and they headed back to the rising waters to search for you. Stones were put in your packs to keep them from being blown into the water by the fierce winds. They had expected that the location of the packs would create a meeting place. A place to set up camp."

"When they returned, unsuccessful, you were all gone, and so were the packs. It may seem too hard to believe, but you have been in hiding ever since the day we tried to speak to the Notus who was with you. We saw him come off of the Middle Meadow and thought he would understand."

Breathing hard, Frank asked, "Is it possible Edalb? Were you missing?"

"Never missing, young Frank, never missing," Edalb replied. "You should step aside. These are not truths."

Instead of stepping out of the way, Frank stepped between Edalb and the stranger. "Edalb, you told me how confusing it was during the big shake. If the water was rising, they had no time to react. Couldn't it have been so confusing for what he just said to be true?"

"Even most of the clan can't tell them apart. To me, they are Orchard Walkers just like you are. Isn't there a small chance that I'm right?"

After speaking, Frank was glad to see that Edalb had lowered his sword… a little.

Frank continued, out of breath, "Besides, you told me that the twig won't work unless I put it back, remember? So, it's no good to them anyway!"

"You do not understand, Frank," Edalb said, continuing to hold his sword at the ready, "An orchard Walker cannot put it back, but anyone else can. They are Notus. If they put the twig back in the tree, the Branch Bridge will rise for them, and they will control the Middle Meadow, the Orchard Walkers will be once again, without a home."

Quartz had raised his sword and was about to swing it at the Enot when Frank held up his hands.

"WAIT!" Frank yelled, "You're saying it will work for them because they aren't Orchard Walkers. I think an Enot was once an Orchard Walker, but a long time ago. Let me prove it to you."

Then he spoke to the Enot. "Enot, I mean Orchard Walker, Subterranean Walker, or whatever you are, if we let you put in the twig and the bridge appears, will you let the Orchard Walkers live out on the Meadow with you?"

"It is what we have always wanted," the Enot said. "We don't want to be blamed for what was done in the past; we want to be back in the clan, working together. We respect to the powers of the Edalb."

Frank turned to Edalb. "Edalb, this has to stop. Let them put the twig back. If the bridge stays down, you will know they are Orchard Walkers, who have been lost from the clan all these years, and not your enemy. If the bridge stays down, then we will all know that I am the only one here who is not an Orchard Walker."

Frank hoped he was doing the right thing when he said, "Let the twig decide."

Edalb was amazed by the events as they happened in front of him and wondered if it all can't be true. *'Maybe it is worth a try,'* he thought to himself, *'But maybe not!'*

"We cannot take the chance, Notus. Stand back!" Stepping forward, both Quartz and Edalb raised their mighty swords once again.

Frank didn't wait, and probably didn't think either, but he grabbed the Enot by the arms that held the twig and pushed him into the tree, as he did, the twig slid evenly into the opening and locked into place.

"Frank!" Edalb yelled, "All is lost! The Meadow will be lost to the Enots!"

"How?" Frank yelled, "Where is the Branch Bridge? Look at the river, nothing is happening! What you call the Enots are not any different from you. They're all Orchard Walkers, Edalb all what you call sub walkers.

You see differences that you created over time. I see them for the first time and see the same Orchard Walker that my grandfather shared with me my whole life." Frank was smiling and yelling all at the same time.

"It is a trick!" said Quartz.

"Edalb, couldn't it be the cycle?" Frank said.

Edalb looked at the small boy. After lowering his sword, he turned to the river. In the reflection of the water, he saw the memory of the boy's grandfather pulling him from the deep water over one hundred years ago and then saw the boy save a stranger just a moment ago.

In the clear water's reflection, Edalb could see the sled from the barn which was the same sled that many cold years ago had begun the journey that again in this warm year began the end of waiting.

Edalb felt his side with his right hand. It was where Frank had laid his head to rest when they hid from these newcomers. Something there was that made this the day to make all days new.

As Edalb turned to look at Frank and the new Orchard Walker, he could see the twig in the knot spinning so slightly. What appeared to be a tight fit was not.

It was waiting for Notus.

Edalb flicked his wrist and the blade he carried turned a shade lighter and silently glided around his waist and rested there, as harmless as a blade of grass.

He said, "And so it is true. The cycle that brought a young boy to the Meadow, the boy that saved my own life so many years ago, now brings this boy, who made the clan whole again.

"You are greater than your years, Notus," Edalb said and turned away and took a few steps. He looked out at the huge gathering around him. Taking a fresh look at the crowd around him he now recognized his clan.

"It is true. A break in the cycle is now repaired. I can feel it in the earth and in the core of the Deep Tree."

Edalb moved toward, and then stood on a small rock and looked about at all the Orchard Walkers around him. Frank could probably not tell, but Edalb saw there were many unfamiliar faces. The crowd had grown larger, and yet he now saw them all as one.

He turned back to the boy by the tree.

"Young Frank," he began, "I, Edalb, carrier of the blade of the Orchard Walker clan, ask you for one small task more. Take the twig from the tree and put it back. For all of us, and I do mean all to see our home, the Middle Meadow at the end of the Branch Bridge."

Frank was not too sure he wanted the journey to end, but knew what he had to do, and so he grabbed the twig slowly from the root of the Deep Tree, and then, with a big smile on his face he put the twig back into the hole that his grandfather had taken it out of, such a long time ago.

When the strange round twig met the knot in the tree, it spun for a moment and seemed to expand, then finding its place, stuck in place.

TWENTY-FOUR

Adam had been quiet while Mom did the dishes. While working at the sink, she stopped to look out the window hoping to see her son running across the yard. The workers had finished at the barn, and she waved as they went back up the hill with the giant spool on the back of their truck.

The Forman of the job came in to apologize about the accident and had told her that from now on, the spools would be kept on their sides, so they wouldn't get away.

"And tell the old man not to worry about the barn. We'll fix it up good as new… well, good as it was anyway. We have some old barn wood from the farm down the road that we knocked down."

She felt bad that she couldn't tell the men what really happened, but the fact that Albert wasn't angry about the destruction to the barn might have given the men enough of a clue to know that it wasn't completely their fault.

TWENTY-FIVE

Not far from where his mother was standing in the kitchen, Frank had just placed the Meadow Twig into the base root of the Deep Tree.

As Frank turned around toward the pond, he exclaimed, “Edalb look! The water’s changing!” But before he could finish, everyone could see what he saw. The Branch Bridge was already coming up from the bottom of the spring.

It looked like a huge arm of an octopus and had even dragged up some weeds from the bottom that hung from it. It was the most awesome thing Frank had ever seen. It started right at the base of the place where he stood and went up like a rainbow over the small stream. From where he was standing, he could not see the other side as it twisted and turned toward the Middle Meadow.

Edalb turned to Frank and said, “Notus, you have taken us all back home. You shall now lead the new clan across the Branch Bridge, back to the Middle Meadow.”

Upon hearing that, all the Orchard Walkers separated and made a path toward the bridge. As Frank made his way to the edge of the river, several of the Orchard Walkers put their mitts out to thank him for bringing them home.

Frank startled several of them by slapping them five. After he did so, they began to slap each other’s hands until it became like a clapping sound all around the bank of the river. It made Frank and several others laugh.

Frank's huge smile was soon replaced by a different face when he started to feel sad. Sad that he knew he would have to go home soon. He missed his family and wanted to know if his brother was okay. And he didn't care if his dad was mad or not.

He turned around at the base of the bridge, wiping a tear out of his eye. "Follow me!" he said, and he started up the side of the bridge.

Edalb came next. Edalb had seen the look on the young boy's face, and as much as he enjoyed Frank, he also knew that Frank was a Notus, and this was not the place for him. Once the clan were safely on the Middle Meadow, he would have to talk to the boy and ask Ria and Quartz to take him home.

One by one, each Orchard Walker took a turn and began stepping up to the base of the bridge. This would be a first time on the meadow for many of them; having been born after the twig was taken from them.

It was as exciting for them as it was for Frank. They also wondered about the meadow, and hoped it was all that they had heard about in the stories that Edalb had told them.

When he reached the top of the bridge, Frank looked around. The small spring that would eventually make its way to the surface of the farm had become almost a river. Frank wondered if the rising bridge had caused the water to change. White swirls and waves could be seen below him. He tried not to look down.

He could just about make out the meadow from here. It was like a lawn in the middle of the river, surrounded by several small trees. *'Weird how a tree can grow underground,'* he thought.

The color of the grass on the meadow matched the Orchard Walkers exactly.

Still pausing at the top of the bridge, Frank turned his head back to face his friends and yelled, “We’re almost there!” and then, because he wasn’t watching his step, Frank slipped on a wet piece of seaweed that had been brought up when the giant root lifted.

Frank tried to reach out for balance, but there was nothing there. As he fell, his head hit the wooden root with a loud ‘THUMP,’ and then he fell, motionless, into the rapids of the river.

Edalb had seen the boy slip and tried to reach out to him but was too late. No one on the bridge could believe it when they saw him slip beneath the waves and not being able to swim, no one could do anything to save him.

Except…

Edalb knelt on the top of the bridge, and tried to see if he could find Frank in the water. Frank was bobbing in and out of the waves as he made his way downstream. Edalb did not think the boy was moving.

With the speed that only the carrier of the blade could use, Edalb once again pulled the blade from around his waist, swinging it high above his head, where the mighty green blade became as hard as steel.

Edalb called on all his power, then yelled with all his might, “BLADE, CUT FOR ME!” and after aiming at the small hero as he bobbed in the waves, Edalb swung the blade twice more around his head then let it fly, hoping that it would find its mark.

After being knocked out by the fall, Frank woke up slightly when he hit the chilly water but could not really move his arms and was having trouble keeping above the rapids as he was carried away.

The last thing Frank heard before going under the water was Edalb yelling in the distance.

But the blade, the blade carried by Edalb; the most powerful of the Orchard Walker clan, flew along the water's surface, gliding toward Frank at remarkable speed as it pierced the tops of the waves seeking its target.

The blade caught up to Frank just as the spring water he was being carried by came out of the ground and entered the small river that ran along Old Rusty.

Exhausted from trying to swim to safety, Frank went under the water, and the blade followed the boy down.

Slipping past Frank's ear, it slid down his shoulder and without cutting any skin, managed to cut the ring of grass that was around Frank's neck. Immediately, the boy grew back to normal size, and lay there, in the river, face down.

TWENTY-SIX

Wanting a minute alone with Adam, and hoping for a better view, Mom went up to the writing room and found Adam standing on a small wooden box, while he concentrated on whatever he could see through the scope.

"See anything, buddy?" she said, hoping for good news.

"Not yet," Adam said. "Hey, you know what Mom? Maybe Grandpa used this thing to spy on the Orchard Walkers in the grass. You can see it really clear. The lawn looks like a jungle through this thing. The same way it looked like when I was small."

When Adam said that he got sad thinking about the adventure he was missing, or maybe also because he did miss his brother a little bit too.

"Can I take a look?" Mom asked. "I had no idea it was that strong, but I suppose if you can see the moon through it..."

Adam stepped off the box and relaxed in the rocking chair. "Sure, take a look." He liked pretending that it was his room.

"Gee, this is neat! It does look like a jungle down there." Then she thought of her son trapped in such a place. "Maybe I can see your father in the woods. How about the river, can you see it from here?"

"Yeah, it's right there," and Adam went over to the window and pointed, "See that shiny piece of water to the left of the woods below Old Rusty? That's the river, by those trees."

Mom had been looking at the woods through the eye piece when she followed Adam's finger and pointed the telescope to the left. She could see where the setting sun was reflecting off the water as it came out of the woods. Even though the river was pretty far off, the telescope brought it up real close.

Mom was having some trouble seeing, and said, "It's tough to focus. The sun keeps getting in my eyes, but I think I see your father… No, wait! Adam, it's Frank! In the river! I see him, he's hurt!"

She continued to yell as she ran out of the room, "Go get your father! Find Grandpa!"

Mom ran out of the house so quickly; Adam had only reached the bottom of the stairs when he heard his mother running down the driveway screaming his brother's name.

When he got to the front porch, he saw his father and granddad coming across the field.

"Mom found Frank! He's hurt!" Then he went running after his mother waving his arms for the men to follow.

As she got to the river edge, Frank's Mother could not control herself. Fearing the worst, she jumped right in, and realized the river at that spot was only a little bit over her shoes. It wasn't deep at all.

"Frank! Frank!" she yelled. "Oh no, was he small, where is he, did I step on him and not know it?"

"Mom?" A voice came from behind a hedge on the bank of the river. "Mom, I'm over here. I'm okay... I think."

She ran to her son and grabbed him, just as Frank's father arrived at the riverbank. He reached down and pulled them both away from the water's edge and hugged his oldest boy.

When Adam came up to the scene, he saw Frank in his father's arms, and his mother kneeling in the grass, crying. She motioned for him to come over, and in one big hug, held both her boys for the first time in what seemed like a lifetime. Grandpa stopped running when he saw that his family was okay.

Looking up at the Deep Tree they called Old Rusty he said, "Thank you, Edalb," and continued towards the family reunion with tears in his eyes.

TWENTY-SEVEN

Dad carried Frank all the way back to the house. Mom wanted him taken right to the car and taken to a doctor, but Frank insisted all he wanted was food and rest. Once upstairs, his mom cleaned the bruise on his head. A lump had begun to form, but the cut was small, so she decided to let Frank rest and look again later.

Frank said it was going to feel great to be in his own bed again, and he was hungry. Adam had so many questions but promised not to bother Frank until after he took a nap.

After he was all washed up, Frank lay in bed surrounded by his family, and he felt sleepy. As Mom lay by his side, his dad carried his clothes in from the bathroom and tossed them on a chair. Grandpa and Adam were there as well.

Frank told his mother that he and the Orchard Walkers had made it all the way to the Middle Meadow, and everyone listened when he shared how the Enots weren't Enots anymore.

Still a bit angry, but relieved that his son was home, Frank's father said, "Now listen, I am so happy that this all turned out as well as it did, but I want a promise from both you and Adam… as a matter of fact, I want Grandpa to promise too, that from this point on you will never try to contact the Orchard Walkers again. We were all lucky, and things could've turned out much worse."

Grandpa got up from sitting on Adam's bed, walked over to the group, and said, "You have our word. Visit again with the Orchard Walkers? Notus!"

Then he winked at Frank and Adam. Adam giggled. Frank's dad had not gotten the joke.

"One more thing." Frank said looking up at his grandfather. "I want to be an Orchard Walker, just like Grandpa."

Adam made a funny face, shook his head, and said, "Grandpa isn't an Orchard Walker. How hard did you hit your head?"

Mom spoke up. "He's tired. He needs to rest. Everyone out!"

But Frank stopped them by saying, "There's more. We're getting the farm back. Edalb says there's no oil, no gas. The gas company will go away."

Frank paused before continuing and said to his grandfather, "When we get it back. I want to learn more about the farm, Grandpa. I want to work with you and be a farmer like you. I see now how important it is. We can make it work."

Frank's grandfather reached down, and with tears in his eyes, started to pat his grandson on his head, and then remembering the bump, touched Frank on the cheek.

"Okay. That would make me incredibly happy."

And then, one by one, the family left the room, until Frank was alone staring at the ceiling. In the squares on the ceiling that were once an imaginary tic-tac-toe board, Frank saw an image as each of the squares in the ceiling became blocks of apple tree varieties that would one day be his orchard.

His future farm staring back at him.

Frank was tired, and so happy to be home again, but he knew he would always wish that he had been able to visit the Middle Meadow and spend more time with his new friends.

Just before falling asleep, he leaned up on his elbows and looked out the window to Old Rusty in the distance, silhouetted by the orange sky. Below the window on the chair where his father had piled his clothes something shiny caught his eye.

As he laid his head down on the pillow, he realized that stuck inside the cloth of his shirt, just below the shoulder, was a small green blade.

It was the blade of the Edalb, carrier of the blade, and leader of the Orchard Walker clan.

About the Author

Frank Geiger spent much of his youth, and the summers of his college years, in Red Hook, N.Y., working the family orchard which was located on Starbarrack Road. If you take a ride, you can still see many of the trees that once made up the original orchard.

Mrs. Shea, the fifth-grade teacher in the story that allowed Albert to write his stories when he was in school, was in real-life this author's fifth grade teacher who saw a young Frank Geiger doodling in class and later allowed him to skip recess from time to time so that he could write his stories about the little creatures that would later become Orchard Walkers.

Frank is now a retired school administrator, and lives in Tennessee.

I hope you enjoyed the Journey to the Middle Meadow with Frank, Ria, Quartz, and Edalb. I wonder if he will ever return to find his sword…

Readers are welcome to email Frank at
orchardwalk@gmail.com.